VENGEANCE

AND

RECKONINGS

VENGEANCE

AND

RECKONINGS

Todd Turner

For Mom and Dad,
the two people who will always have the most
powerful influence on my life.

I miss you every day.

PROLOGUE

A blinding flash followed by a vacuum in space that seemed to stop time, silence, then an expansion of air, with a percussive force so massive it signaled the end of everything. For the people in this moment in this place in the universe, it *was* the end of everything. A force so strong and powerful, it seemed it could only have come from God Himself.

He had been envisioning this scene for years. *His* drive—no, his obsession—was to bring an epic devastation upon the United States. *He* is Mohammad Omar Kundi, and he vehemently hated America. He hated everything it stood for, especially secularism. In his mind, no country should exist that isn't guided by a specific religious faith in its laws and institutions, and any such nation should be destroyed.

The phone call from his daughter made him smile. An instrument to be played, she was playing her part to his immense satisfaction. This operation was now in its final stage, his dream becoming reality.

This plan had consumed him, every hour day and night. He alone was the mastermind that managed to convince North Korea's unpredictable leader to pull resources from developing an ICBM capable of delivering a nuclear warhead to the United States. Kundi explained to Kim Jong-un how improbable it was such a missile would ever reach American territory, even if North Korea could obtain the necessary material to build such a bomb. Kundi had a better plan: Iran would supply enriched plutonium and technical expertise to build the bombs, and North Korea would get those bombs installed in factory-fresh cars destined for the United States. While Kim despised the idea of sharing the glory with Iran, the prospect of causing such terror and devastation proved irresistible.

Brilliantly—and Kundi certainly thought so—his plan even had contingencies to thwart an investigation and stymie efforts of U.S. authorities to interfere were the plot somehow discovered. That contingency had cost millions, but Kundi viewed it simply as an expensive insurance policy.

Mohammad Kundi thought back to the time he had taken his daughter Rezeya, and left his wife for dead. He certainly had no idea then what an asset she would become. Her indoctrination began as a child, and at age twelve she had been relocated to a suburb of Detroit. Her identity as an immigrant from Pakistan would be carefully cultivated. Rezeya would get a PhD in mathematics, a marriage of convenience and a position at General Motors—where she would be instrumental in the final phase of the plan. Even so, Rezeya was near to fulfilling her destiny, and her father would determine that her purpose on this earth would come to a conclusion soon.

JUNE 25, 09:42 PDT

Port of Benicia, California

The onetime capital for the State of California, Benicia was founded by three men. Comandante General Mariano Guadalupe Vallejo, one of those three, wished to name the city after his wife, Francisca, but his choice was rejected when the nearby Yerba Buena coincidentally changed its name to San Francisco. So, the city along the north bank of the murky Carquinez Straight, which connects the Sacramento River to the pristine San Francisco Bay, became known as Benicia: a place where even on a sunny day feels lazy, gray, and somewhat gloomy. The tiny Port of Benicia is so small that it gets barely a mention in any of the city's promotional literature, and to find it by car you need precise directions. Some streets leading to the port area are now blocked off with a fence, changes implemented for the *appearance* of security— the theater of post-9/11 "safety."

The Benicia deep-water pier, primarily used as a vehicle processing facility for both Toyota and General Motors, allows the berthing of up to three vessels simultaneously, though no one there can remember such an occasion. Currently owned by the international company AMPORTS, the Benicia port is but one of eleven ports the company operates for the purpose of auto importing and processing for distribution.

General Motors uses this facility for the importation of cars built at the Korean factories it acquired when they picked the carcass of the bankrupt Korean automobile manufacturer Daewoo Motors.

On this damp, cold and gray morning, the Norwegian-flagged *Trinidad*, a massive specialty vehicle transport ship of the Wallenius Wilhelmsen Line, was docked at the port. One by one, brand-new cars were coming out of the bowels of the ship, down a ramp, driven by longshoremen, and parked neatly in a paved area, along the water's edge, called the *first place of rest*. From here, each car is processed for inland transportation, either by rail or truck, to a franchised Chevrolet dealer somewhere in the United States.

These port processing centers have extensive capabilities: their full-service body shop can repair almost any damage the cars may have suffered on the journey across the ocean, and they install accessories from radios to spoilers to optional wheels and tires. The most important service, though, is the quality/predelivery inspection (PDI) each car goes through before being sent to the dealer. GM employs seventeen inspectors at the Benicia Terminal to perform this service.

Twenty-three-year-old Carl Johnson, one such inspector, was frustrated. As a fully trained and certified ASE (Automotive Service Excellence) and GM-certified mechanic, he was always pissing and moaning about not having any real mechanic's work to do. Just once he'd like to overhaul an engine or rebuild a transmission. Yet working on cars fresh from the factory, the chances of this happening were next to none. It was with such an attitude that carried him through the PDI for the new Chevy Spark now before him.

A simple thing like discovering a defective fuel gauge wouldn't present a difficult challenge, but at least it was something more than the usual check-off-the-boxes routine. There are three possibilities for a faulty fuel gauge reading on all cars, modern and old: the sending unit in the gas tank isn't sending a signal; the gauge is not capable of receiving and displaying the signal; or there is a lost connection in the wiring somewhere between the two devices.

Once Carl verified the fuel gauge in the dash was working and the wired connection was in working order, he went on to the more time-consuming process of inspecting the sending unit located in the gas tank.

As is common practice, the access point is under the rear seat cushion, which is removed simply by removing two small bolts, then pulling up on the back of the cushion to release two clips holding it in place. With the seat removed, a small plate secured to the "floor" of the car is visible.

Once the plate is removed, you can see the wires and tubes coming from the gas tank. They're attached to a circular plate mounted to the tank with four screws. A rubber gasket is visible around the edges of the plate.

Ordinarily, this is one of the easier parts replacements to accomplish: unplug the wire connectors, remove the screws, pull out the defective part, remove it from the retainer and reverse the process. Or at least that's how it's supposed to go.

When Carl pulled out the device, however, he was confused. It just didn't look at all like what he expected. While the part was the same one he had pulled off the shelf to install, something was attached to it that shouldn't have been there.

Initially, he hardly noticed the small extra wire coming off the lead from the nylon plug on the outside of the gas tank. Now, seeing a thick vinyl-coated wire leading down from the fuel pump into the gas tank, he backed up and looked again at the connector on the outside of the tank—where he saw a flexible rubberized antenna. He thought out loud, "Why would the gas tank need an antenna?"

Carl sat staring at the additional wiring, but no matter how long he stared at it he was no closer to figuring it out. He went back to the wire attached to the fuel pump that led into the gas tank. As he gently pulled on the wire, it became taut. He pulled a little harder and something felt as though it slipped out of a friction connector. He slackened the wire . . . and something clanged in the bottom of the tank and he felt the wire tense. Curious now, he resumed pulling on the wire, estimating that whatever it was attached to was at least fifteen pounds.

Then he saw under the vinyl coating a braided wire—braided to offer enough strength to support the weight of the device attached to it.

Seeing something shiny through the access hole, Carl turned on the small LED lamp on his safety glasses to look into the tank. What he saw was the wire leading down to a perfectly machined cylinder made of some type of very shiny metal. It wasn't aluminum or steel. It didn't even look like titanium.

At this point Carl was no longer curious, he was just confused. He very carefully pulled the cylinder out and laid it down on a shop towel. It was nearly the same diameter as the access hole, about five and a half inches, and about ten inches long. Then it all came together for Carl: the antenna, the cylinder, the thick wire; and Carl whispered, "Is this a bomb?"

He had no clue what kind of bomb, or even if it *was* a bomb; it could be something made to look like a bomb by someone to cause a scare. One thing Carl was damn good at, though, was not jumping to conclusions when he didn't have all the answers.

Pacing around the car now, Carl kept repeating to no one, "What do I freaking do?" Other mechanics were around, working on similar tasks; and, as always when confronted with a problem, it's comforting to bring someone in on it.

Carl approached Jim and genially asked, "Hey, Jim, ah . . . will you take a look at this?"

They all helped one another out from time to time and Jim was appreciative of the break in routine. "Whatcha got, man?"

"Not sure. I found this attached to the fuel gauge sender. It felt like it was seated to a clip or something in the bottom of the gas tank."

Jim climbed in the car for a closer look. He first suggested just cutting the wire and getting rid of it, but as he got a closer look he exclaimed, "Damn! Looks like a bomb or something, man."

"Yeah, but why? Who'd put a fucking bomb in a car?"

Backing away from the car, Jim mumbled, "Fuck me, dude. I don't have a clue, and I sure as hell don't wanna get involved with this clusterfuck."

Carl decided in that moment, *Screw it. If I'm wrong, I'll be treated like a low-grade idiot. If I'm right, well . . . Who knows?* There wasn't much of a downside. Carl left his work area, found a place he felt sure he could get a clear signal, and dialed 911.

After being hung up on twice by the 911 operator as a crank caller, he decided to call the FBI directly—which wasn't exactly a slam dunk either. Who would have thought in the post-9/11 era it would be so hard to report something suspicious? It took a determination of purpose Carl didn't know he had. The fifth person Carl talked to at last began to take him seriously, at least seriously enough to ask where he was.

JUNE 25, 11:08 PDT

Port of Benicia, California

After Carl carefully described what he'd seen, where he was, and what kind of car the device was in, the agent sat quietly, processing what he'd been told. Derrick Porter was a new agent in the San Francisco field office. With a GS11 pay scale, he wasn't a grunt, but he wasn't explicitly in charge of anything, either. Such calls came in seldom but with enough regularity they were not unheard of; yet this one piqued his interest. He decided to head down to the port himself and logged in the call at 11:15 A.M. He also decided to go alone. When Derrick arrived at the port operations it was 12:09 P.M.

Carl met him at the front gate in his car. The complex was large and lacked signage, almost every building identical in construction and industrial beige color. Derrick followed in his FBI-issued Ford Taurus.

As they walked into the garage, all hell broke loose. Carl's boss, Dick—a name everyone thought described the man to a T—was a miserable example of a human being. He was standing by the ripped-apart car, ranting about where was that fucking worthless waste of skin now, throwing tools and having a fit like a four-year-old. Just as he was about to reach in and grab the fuel gauge sending unit, Carl hollered, "Hey, Dick, back off, man! I am working on that. Leave it alone if you know what's good for you."

Carl's threat pushed Dick over the edge. Dick hated just about everyone, but he especially hated *blacks*, *spics*, and *homos*. He never shied from using epithets long since abandoned by civilized society, and none of those so described would ever dare tell him to back off. He jumped back and spun around—all 5-foot-7 and 240 apoplectic pounds of him—about to tear out Carl's jugular when he noticed Derrick.

Derrick came off as a metrosexual to anyone with any degree of worldliness, but to someone like Dick he was a *fag*, period. Men like Dick always thought they knew, and Derrick wasn't about to give him any confirmation, either way.

Dick spat out, "That's it, you've done it. Get your lazy black ass and your nigger ass–loving faggot boyfriend out of here! You're fucking fired!" Dick fired people daily, but it didn't mean they were fired; he just loved to intimidate people, and what better intimidation is there? Everyone would just ignore him and show up for work the next day as usual.

Derrick didn't know this—nor would it have mattered if he had. He pulled his badge with one hand while sliding his coat to the side to expose his gun with the other, using the voice he'd been taught at Quantico. "FBI. You are on the verge of interfering in a federal investigation. Would you honestly like to try your hand with me, buddy?" Derrick waited for a response. "Yeah, that's what I thought: all bark. Now slowly step away from the car and turn your back toward me."

Dick actually *was* stupid enough to respond with a full-throated "Fuck off!"

"You think this is a joke, asshole?" Derrick demanded. He approached Dick and the moment Dick turned, Derrick kicked the back of his left knee, collapsing him to the floor. With Dick down, Derrick hissed, "Now put your hands on the back of your head and hold still." Derrick cuffed him and helped him stand up.

Dick grumbled about being read his rights, to which Derrick bluntly informed him, "You're a suspect in a potential terrorism case, dumb-ass, and if you're as ignorant as I think you are, you've probably never heard of the Patriot Act. Let me summarize it for you: you don't have any rights!"

Derrick jerked him over to a hip-high "railing" made of a three-inch red pipe planted in the cement floor at both ends to protect the shop's equipment from an errant car. Using a zip tie from the shop, Derrick secured the chain on the handcuffs to the pipe barricade.

Satisfied that Dick would no longer offer an opinion, Derrick stepped back over to the car where Carl now stood with eyes wide and the merest hint of a grin. Derrick snapped him back to reality. "Show's over. What do you have here?"

Carl was in his element, explaining something he knew about. He showed Derrick the cylinder, then detailed the odd wire and how it looked like an antenna, then the high-strength wire.

Derrick felt his skin turn to ice, his heart raced to where he thought he was having a heart attack, and he struggled to keep down his breakfast burrito. He'd never had a panic attack and felt like he was going to die.

No doubt about it, this looked like a bomb. Question was, what kind of bomb? It was too well made: perfectly machined, a brightly finished cylinder with perfectly welded end caps such that the welds weren't even visible; no way could this be an amateur job or a hoax. Also, the metal looked to be zirconium, a metal used in nuclear reactors. Its low-capture neutron cross-section made it highly effective at shielding radiation. By pure coincidence, Derrick had seen zirconium on a field trip as a kid when they'd toured a nuclear reactor.

Derrick called his bosses' boss, Charlene Thornton, the Special Agent In Charge at the San Francisco office. This was no high school pipe bomb prank. This bomb was expensive, of that he was certain. He had a hell of a time reaching Special Agent Thornton, and when he did, he received a lecture about proper channels—but when he was able to brief her on the details of the bomb, the lecture was over.

Wishing to preempt another dressing down, Derrick then told her he planned to call someone he knew and respected at the CIA. At that point he had to hold the phone away from his ear. At very high decibels Thornton screamed, "You goddamn well better be joking! If you do any such thing, you'll be lucky to find a job as a security guard at the mall. Am I making myself clear?"

"With all due respect," Derrick responded, "I'm not asking for your permission, I'm giving you a heads-up, and will face the consequences as you deem appropriate."

Thornton, taking note of his respectful tone and candor, then replied, "You're making a hell of a gamble." When Derrick didn't reply, she added, "I'll see you ASAP."

Derrick taped off the area around the car and asked everyone to leave the building, then nodded to Dick for him to give his consent. Forty-six minutes later, Thornton and two other agents, one with a Geiger counter, were on the scene via helicopter. The sick feeling in Derrick's stomach had not gone away.

Derrick's other call could have dire consequences on his career; it would blow protocol and chain of command to hell. Yet contacting Craig Stout was precisely what his gut told him. Scrolling through his phone, he found the email address Craig had given him when he'd attended a special training course at the CIA's "Farm" the previous summer.

JUNE 25, 15:42 EDT

Washington, D.C.

There is nothing like the bureaucracy of Washington, D.C., to mire the progress of anything.

"I swear to God this place is a black hole where time and decisions go to die a slow death. What should take a few minutes for a person of action takes an eternity in this city," proclaimed an exasperated Craig Stout as he exited the committee room of the Capitol Building.

This was exactly like every other briefing by the Subcommittee on Terrorism/HUMINT, Analysis and Counterintelligence, the congressional committee charged with oversight of the nation's sixteen intelligence operations. Even though Craig wasn't a ranking director for any of these agencies, he was frequently asked to provide a picture of what he was experiencing in the field, an unfiltered analysis of threat and assessment.

Craig always felt these sessions were a waste of time. No one in Congress had a clue about just how ugly the world of intelligence is, nor would they have the stomach for it if they did. They thought *politics* was brutal; hah! Unlike politics, his business didn't involve swaying to the whims of the public. He preferred to have a direction and stick to it—well aware this dog-headedness was both asset and liability.

The president himself had instigated Craig's involvement in these briefings. Both the committee and Craig were less than enthusiastic supporters of that idea, which matters little when the request comes from the Oval Office. As for Craig, he went along as a favor to a friend.

Craig realized president John Barton had won office in an extremely tight election: the third such event in two decades; and without a mandate, the president is something of a lame duck going into office—especially when partisans on the other side of the aisle will do and say anything to stymie progress. Craig suspected nothing was lost on Barton, who, with such a keen intellect and an amazing ability to read between the lines, probably would have been better suited as the director of the CIA.

John Barton hadn't spent decades in political life before becoming president. As a one-and-a-half-term governor of Colorado and erstwhile mayor of Colorado Springs, he'd been anything but a shoo-in for president. His lack of political experience and his direct, Western approach to addressing the issues, though, made him particularly appealing to a wide swath of the electorate. In many ways, he was an intellectual Democratic version of George W. Bush, who had won on his affable good ol' boy demeanor. Bush's two terms had left the country with no shortage of enemies around the world.

One of the president's two sons, Scott, had been friends with Craig Stout since Craig and his family had moved to Colorado Springs when he was in junior high. Scott and Craig immediately hit it off and began spending most of their free time together. Biking, hiking, kayaking, camping, fishing, snowboarding, they were outdoor enthusiasts seizing every opportunity to be outside.

There were additional reasons for this type of activity aside from the fact they both enjoyed the outdoors so much. Being away from the prying eyes of their respective families also gave them the opportunity to explore their intimate feelings for each other. They felt their families would never understand; and even at a young age, they were astute enough to understand the value of "keeping the peace."

Being gay wasn't something either of them accepted with ease. They both resisted their desires and fought against their feelings. Scott's family was always progressive thinking. His parents had gay friends, and gay couples, men and women, were in his life and around him since his childhood. For Scott, there was no barrier to believing that two men or two women could love each other. He feared, though, what his peers would think of him. His desire to be accepted among them was important to Scott—that is, until Craig convinced him their classmates had even less of a clue about what was important to their future lives than they did.

As for Craig, accepting he was gay would take another decade. It would require undoing and redefining instilled perceptions of manhood and what manly behavior was. Ideas ingrained in his psyche from careless comments made over the years by his cement contractor father would make him feel that being gay was not just wrong but degrading.

After high school, both decided to pursue their own paths, especially when it came to college. They, Craig more than Scott, foolishly thought the physical separation might somehow prove they were just infatuated kids and would outgrow their desires.

NOVEMBER 8, 2006

Los Angeles, CA

A phone ringing in the middle of the night is never good news, even in a frat house, where activity doesn't necessarily end at what mature people consider a civilized hour. Four A.M., though, is late even for hormone-driven youth with inhibitions numbed by alcohol to be calling their buds, totally incognizant of the time.

It was such a call, on this November night, unusually warm as a result of the gusty Santa Ana winds, that would forever change the course of Craig's life. Through the muddled fog of sleep, Craig identified a deep gravelly voice that said he was with the Arizona Highway Patrol. Craig recalled initially being annoyed, having been awakened and failing to find the context of why this guy might be calling. After all, he was in California, and couldn't think of why the Arizona Highway Patrol would be calling him.

Just as the cobwebs were beginning to clear, his heart skipped when he remembered his parents were driving from Colorado to visit. The official-sounding voice asked, "Is this Craig Stout? Are you the son of Richard and Nancy Stout?"

Craig had a feeling of dread so intense it produced a terror that began at his throat and spread rapidly down to his gut and swept over him, sending a cold sweat down his spine completely at odds with the warmth of the night. He swallowed the lump in his throat and responded, "Yes, sir."

After a pause the officer continued. "Mr. Stout, this is Major Tom Reynolds. Your parents were involved in an accident on the scenic route between Flagstaff and Sedona, in Oak Creek Canyon. It would seem that a car traveling the other direction was in their lane as your parents rounded a turn. It looks like your father swerved to avoid a collision, but lost control of the vehicle. There is no easy way to say this. Their motor home went through the guardrail and down the ravine. It took rescue teams a little over two hours to reach the wreckage . . . I'm sorry. Your parents are deceased. There was nothing anyone could do."

That conversation would play out like a sickening movie in his mind over the years, like a dream, just a vague collection of memories. This was how Craig Stout learned he had become an orphan—not as one begging for a bowl of porridge, but as an only child, for the first time in his life, well and truly alone. The panic and ensuing sorrow gave him two epiphanies: that this horrible feeling of sinking into darkness is reserved solely for those whom the deceased leave behind; and that recognizing this fear for what it is allowed him to get control of that feeling. He now knew death was nothing to fear. It is living that is difficult and at times almost unbearably painful— and at the same time, paradoxically, beautiful.

NOVEMBER 12, 2006

Denver, Colorado

The memorial was awkward. Craig and his grandparents (on his mother's side), and his dad's brother, Uncle Bill, were the sole survivors. Uncle Bill took over planning the service and reception, leveraging the Stouts' relationship with the governor, and the service was held at St. Paul Lutheran Church, one block north of the capitol building in downtown Denver. Governor Barton, along with his wife, Elizabeth, and their sons Trent and Scott were there, sitting in the second pew behind the family. Craig hadn't seen Scott in a little over two years, and while they still talked on the phone and exchanged email, even that had dwindled in the past several months.

When Craig proceeded into the chapel to take his place in the first pew, he saw Scott standing in the row behind; now he knew he would make it through the day. He couldn't manage a smile, but Scott could tell from his calmer expression that Craig was pleased to see him. As Craig sat, Scott reached forward and gave Craig's shoulder a firm squeeze. The soft "Thank you," whispered in a sigh, was a clear signal that the gesture was very much appreciated.

What followed, for Craig, was a blur. Walking away seemed surreal. *What, I just leave them here?* was all he could think as he moved from the grave toward the limo, anxious and yet reticent to leave.

The governor had offered the governor's mansion for the reception. Even though Craig always suspected Scott's father knew—or at least had a suspicion of the true nature of his friendship with his son—it was clear that the man who would become president had a sense that Craig was in some way good for his son.

Scott, for his part, never had the kind of love-hate relationship so prevalent with political families, partly because his dad hadn't planned to enter politics. He was a businessman—and a damn good one—one of the few CEOs who had the respect and admiration of employees and stockholders alike.

The Colorado Democratic Party recruited him specifically to run for governor against a Republican incumbent. He genuinely thought they all had lost their marbles. Turns out that the party had a wildcard up their sleeve, a piece of dirt that would bury the opponent. They could have run a chimpanzee and won with the dirty bomb they had.

Had Barton ever known of the plan, he would have had nothing to do with it. Once elected, though, he decided to do what he could to spearhead cleaning up the electoral process, at least in the state of Colorado.

Scott's respect for his father, at a level of maturity uncommon at his age, is what kept him from feeling the need to have his relationship with Craig acknowledged by his dad. That and the minor detail that he never honestly knew what the hell the relationship was to begin with. Scott and Craig were friends, and yes, they had been intimate, but he never considered Craig a boyfriend, mostly because he feared his true feeling would ultimately be unrequited.

They trusted each other. They were in many ways more like brothers in the way they felt, except for, of course, those times they were intimate. Even then, it was the time afterward, when they were completely relaxed and calm, that they shared their greatest fears, and also their greatest hopes. That pillow talk is always when they felt closest.

This unspoken acceptance of the relationship kept things on an even keel. While both young men knew they couldn't have the live-in relationship most couples assume, they also managed to convince themselves that neither wanted that, at least not yet.

During the reception, the governor approached and asked Craig if he could have a chat with him in his office down the hall. Walking into the office, Craig noticed a man in one of the brown leather club chairs. Barton's office looked more like a gentlemen's club, or a dark cigar bar. It exuded masculinity, with its deep, rich colors, heavy furniture and thick rugs; a great place for men to bond. Governor Barton said, "Craig, I'd like you to meet Mr. Pecone. He's with the CIA."

What Craig didn't learn until later was that Pecone was the CIA's most successful recruiter. For the past two years Pecone had been stalking Craig, his dream recruit. Pecone saw Craig as a vital, intelligent, physical man with secrets and the deep-seated need to prove something, in no small part because of those secrets.

So, Pecone convinced the governor to arrange the introduction. Barton was so appalled and disgusted with the timing (he called it "piss-poor judgment" to do it at the funeral) that he wanted no part and made that clear by leaving the room.

Craig later learned that with a track record of finding not just officers but the most talented operatives in the agency's roster, *golden* was the term used to describe any of Pecone's recruits at the CIA's training facility, affectionately called "the farm."

Pecone's fame was such that he was even portrayed in Hollywood films, much to the chagrin of the CIA, an organization that zealously guards its secrecy. One of several agency recruiters, Pecone was, in terms of numbers, the lowest producer of trainees. He preferred to research his recruits, know their character faults and what made them tick, and most especially, what vulnerabilities could be leveraged and manipulated by the agency.

His recruits were usually singled out for worse treatment at the CIA's not-so-secret training camp nestled in the Virginia woods. In a high-stakes version of internecine politics, camp trainers felt it necessary to break one of Pecone's special recruits, as a way to show him up. And it all occurred, of course, behind the backs of those responsible for the camp's operation. In a twisted irony it was precisely this treatment that made Pecone's officers the success they were.

Pecone called himself a *people reader* but not in some supernatural way; rather, he could pick up on subtle clues, the ones most people can't see. Pecone was intensely proud of his ability to learn a few basic facts, then see into a person's soul: to know unerringly what made that person tick. Of course, there weren't many whom Pecone would call friends. Most found his unique abilities disarming and downright spooky, not to mention invasive and annoying. His talent was great for recruiting spooks, but not so much for a social life.

Craig's being gay was, of course, the secret. Pecone saw that as both a liability and an asset: while he could keep a secret—clearly an asset—the liability was that Craig also had something to prove. As a young man growing up gay in Colorado, no doubt he would be insecure and feel conflicted about the expectations of who he was supposed to be. Yeah, that could be used.

Pecone could tell that Craig's intelligence was far beyond what standard tests show even though his methods are not recognized and established. Sure, he'd received good grades all through school, but anyone who applied himself can do that. Study the material given. Take the test on the material given, and voila! You're a 4.0 student.

The intelligence needed to be a good operative, however, is demonstrated by a person's ability to reason, and discover the story out of pieces of information, and develop assessments based on observations and logic, not just an ability to remember facts. Tests had been developed to measure these abilities as well, but Pecone didn't need a test. He could see it, and Craig had it.

Pecone didn't try to make friends with new recruits and then spring on them this idea of an incredible opportunity. His approach was more direct. He asked Craig straight out, "Don't you want to do something with your life?"

Craig stood there in shock, feeling both insulted and called out; mostly, though, he was disquieted by the fact that Mr. Pecone was right. He *didn't* feel that he was doing anything important with his life.

Had Craig known then what he later learned, he'd understand that recruiters for secretive government agencies tend to focus on introducing the idea of "contributing" to the nation at a time when their recruits are most vulnerable emotionally. That includes as well right after an attack, as on September 11. When that went down, hundreds of people rushed into recruiting offices desperately wanting to "do something."

Pecone (if that was even his name, which Craig thought doubtful) started by expressing his deep-felt condolences for Craig's loss.

"I know you are feeling a bit lost at sea, both literally and figuratively. A loss like you've just encountered shakes the very foundation of your life. You no longer feel grounded. I am deeply sorry."

Craig was taken aback. He'd heard at least a hundred condolences over the last few days but nothing like that. He quietly responded with a thank you and then awkwardness, as he couldn't understand who this stranger was or why he was here.

Recruitment candidates—that is, if they are worth two bits—will always view the gregarious approach of a stranger with suspicion. People don't just express an interest in you and your life without wanting something. Craig would give Pecone that *what the hell do you want?* look, and though Craig couldn't have known it, Pecone wasn't disappointed.

When the recruiter invited Craig out for a drink, he could smell the suspicion.

"Let me explain," said Pecone. "I want to pitch you something. An offer, actually."

Ever the skeptic and always slow to lower his guard, Craig's "Yeah, really?" wasn't so much disrespectful as it was closed off. He wasn't much for letting people through his barriers these days.

Pecone's *humph* was his only answer. It meant, "Yeah, I know you want to close yourself off from everyone right now, but you'll soon realize if you keep wallowing in self-pity the rut you've put yourself in." The message wasn't lost.

"Sorry ... I'm just impatient and a little distrustful these days. What's the offer?"

Deciding on the spot, Pecone came right out and told him. "I am a recruiter for the CIA, and not to be boastful, but my officers are some of the best the agency has. They're all going high places."

"Sounds exciting and interesting, but I've never thought of myself as James Bond or anyone like him, and when it comes to living under the confines of military like discipline, that's definitely not my style."

"I wish I could promise you the adventure-packed thrill of being James Bond. The problem is, he's a fictional character. Being an operative, especially in this day and age, is neither romantic nor exciting. It's terror-filled and messy."

Craig laughed. "So where's the opportunity part of this? You make it sound horrible. You're not much of a recruiter."

"It actually gets worse. You'll risk your life. You'll wallow in mud. You'll get beat up and maybe even tortured. You'll have to live with the guilt of killing people, and no one but a key few will ever have any idea what you've done. It's not likely anyone will ever thank you. In fact, most of the people you work for will disavow ever even knowing you, especially if the shit hits the fan."

With a private chuckle that somehow escaped, Craig said, "Sounds like the job mucking the stalls I was sold on as a kid, but I'm not a kid anymore. I know there isn't a pony in all that shit."

"I'm banking on it. I'm also counting on your deeply seated need to prove a point, accomplish things that are said to be impossible, and show the world just how narrow-minded their prejudices are."

"Not really! I don't give a rat's ass what the world thinks of me."

"Christ, boy, I hadn't realized you'd taken up lying to yourself, too! That's the biggest crock of shit I've heard in a long while," said Pecone in a huff. "If you didn't give a damn, you would have never bothered even trying to stay in the closet. Discretion wouldn't even have been a remote concern of yours."

"Maybe I just don't see myself as a raving queen, flitting about like a caricature from a BBC dramedy."

"Look, I'm not here to debate, I'm here to find talent. I see it in you, and when you have a chance to think it through, I hope to hear from you."

Craig slipped the offered card in his coat pocket with barely a glance. His intentions were to forget he'd ever met this whack job, get home and hit the weights and treadmill hard enough so he would be too exhausted to even think about this day, his parents' death, or this last taxation on his mind, Pecone.

NOVEMBER 12, 2006

Denver, Colorado

Craig accepted the invitation from the Bartons to stay at the governor's mansion without much thought given to the prospect of reconnecting with Scott. While he thought he would be less likely to want that—given the circumstances of his being in Colorado—the truth was quite the opposite.

He didn't even know what drew him to Scott's door, but there he was gently knocking. Scott opened it, hoping to see Craig, and as he went to invite Craig into an embrace, he found Craig coming to him, nearly knocking him down, wrapping his arms around him. He felt steadied once again with the strength of Craig's body holding him in a tight embrace.

It all happened so quickly, and as Scott began to wrap his arms around his friend, he felt Craig's head drop—and then deep, deep sobbing. This had never been their dynamic. Craig was always stoic and firm; at times Scott wondered if he had any emotions at all. This was a moment that bonded the two men. They knew they were more than just friends, and now it was obvious that their needs went far beyond sex as well.

As Craig's sobs weakened, Scott gently guided him into bed, where for the first time they truly made love. It was tender, slow, longing, and deeply satisfying, leaving them both spent and yet too excited to sleep.

As they lay in bed they began to talk. They made plans for how they would define their relationship, how they would maneuver the coming separation they would face. Craig told Scott about his meeting with Pecone. Scott, of course, knew of the offer and hoped more than ever that Craig would accept it. The CIA training camp was only a short drive from Scott's chosen university.

"So, what do you think of the idea of becoming an operative for the CIA"? asked Scott with both honest curiosity and—notably—newfound concern for his safety.

Craig was still slow on picking up the subtle cues, but this one he got. "Well, honestly, I was a little pissed off at having this dude throw this at me at the time he did. But as I thought more, something about it made sense, and even seemed exciting."

Scott murmured, "Um hum."

Craig pulled Scott's body closer. "You didn't let me finish. I also now feel it's not just my decision but one I would want to hear your opinion about too, understanding this will affect you too."

Scott was moved to tears, "I can't tell you how happy that makes me, that you'd already consider my feelings on this."

"I guess I've had to do a lot of growing up this past week, and if events tonight told me anything, it was that I've been lying to myself about my feelings for you and, well, for guys in general."

"Yeah, there's been a lot of that going around the past few days; as to the job, I know how dangerous it would be, and the worst part is, often I'd not even be able to know what you're doing—but I trust you, and I know I love you, so in the end I'd want to support anything you feel strongly about doing."

Craig heard the words, and as strongly as he felt for Scott in this moment, he couldn't bring himself to say *I love you*—it scared him still, but also it felt too early.

QUANTICO, VA MARCH 2017

Camaraderie

A decade later, in the spring of 2017, Craig found himself at a lectern at the FBI's training farm in Quantico, VA, giving an assessment of the cadets' latest training exercise, one he was brought in to conduct as an expert in the field. While there may or may not be a "gay mafia" subculture in America, gay people tend to favor someone from the "tribe" if all else is just about equal. Any group considered or believes itself to be an outlier from the mainstream will find like others and build connections, trusting one another more easily, whether that trust is well-founded or not.

When those in the community are closeted, sometimes these connections are never acknowledged; rather they are assumed, with this wildly inaccurate sense known as *gaydar*. This was the situation with Craig and Derrick Porter.

Craig had impressed so many of the instructors at the farm that he was frequently invited back, and, on occasion, was also a guest lecturer at Quantico. Derrick attended one such lecture and felt that familiar vibe. He suspected, or maybe hoped, that Craig might be "one of his kind." He'd taken a chance, introduced himself, and asked if he could keep in touch with Craig. "You know, just maybe get some pointers or something," was his nervously flustered explanation. Craig, of course, being an instructor (and also being Craig) wouldn't outwardly confirm or deny Derrick's suspicions. That connection is frequently unspoken, like the lift of an eyebrow.

Such as it was, Craig thus had given Derrick his CIA card. Whether either realized it, the subtle smile or even upward turn of the corners of their eyes was enough to signal they were on the right track. Craig listed no title on his card, no mention he was with the CIA, just the name *Craig Stout* with a handwritten phone number. That number rang only to a communications center where a message could be left, but he wrote out his personal email address on the card. Without saying a word, Derrick understood this was extraordinary.

If he only understood how that number soon would be used!

There had been another reason Derrick asked for Craig's card: he found him incredibly attractive, and at the end of training he made his move, sending Craig an email with an invitation to a celebratory drink the following Saturday evening.

Craig read the email suspiciously. *Hi Craig, I hope it's not presumptuous of me to use your first name. I wanted to see if you'd be interested in getting together for a drink tomorrow night. The last weeks of training have been intensely brutal, and I would very much enjoy the chance to celebrate the occasion of making it through this hell hole.* It was signed, *thanks much, Derrick.*

Had Derrick been in the class one year ago, Craig might have been much more tempted. He and Scott had been going through a rough time, the years of Craig's secretiveness taking their toll. The turning point was when Scott, now at the NSA, gained security clearance even above Craig's. Now they could talk, and while it was now Scott couldn't tell him certain things, Craig was far more accommodating to such secrets—as long as they related to work. He could compartmentalize that.

Craig decided he'd meet with Derrick, and though tempted, was very committed to Scott and planned to let Derrick down easy.

Derrick had chosen a bar near the farm that was not at all gay but was known to be discreet, with booths that afforded some level of privacy. Craig arrived and Derrick waved him over to his booth. Before Craig could even offer his hand to shake, Derrick embraced him with both arms.

"Thanks for coming, I'm sure glad to see you."

Trying to keep it casual, Craig said, "Yeah sure, let's have a seat," wanting to put some table distance between them.

Derrick didn't sense the rebuffing, too excited at the prospect of where the evening might lead. They ordered two beers and a specialty appetizer to share. When the beers arrived, Derrick offered a toast. "To new acquaintances." They clanked glasses and took a sip; but when Craig felt Derrick's hand cover his own on the table, he knew he'd have to stop this earlier than he hoped.

Pulling back his hand, he looked Derrick in the eyes. "You are an incredibly hot guy, and I'd be lying if I said I wasn't interested, but the fact is I have a partner, who I've just been through a rough patch with, but I'm very much in love with him."

Derrick was embarrassed, telling himself, *You idiot, you should have known someone like Craig would be taken.* He made some excuse, muttering, "Yeah, that's what I figured, it's cool, I just wondered, that's all." He wanted to leave at that point but stayed for a few more minutes, asking for the check. Craig insisted on paying, so Derrick wouldn't feel bad or foolish, telling him, "Look, doesn't mean we can't keep in touch."

Derrick knew that it meant exactly that.

JUNE 25, 15:44 EDT

Washington, D.C.

Luckily, Craig was in the country when his phone popped up an email notice. The panicked message from Derrick read, Hello Craig, Unfortunately, I am writing you because I need something. This is so urgent, I am actually terrified, and know I am in way over my head. I hope you get this message soon. I have to move FAST! Please call on secured lines as soon as you read this message.

Annoyed at first (*Why the hell do I only hear from people when they need something?*), Craig wasn't going to let Derrick stew. That he wrote at all said a lot: this was business. He picked up the phone, a secure line. The outgoing caller ID read 999-555-1212, a number reserved by the phone companies to never be assigned.

"Derrick here."

"Yeah, Derrick, this is Craig, are you on a secure phone?"

Derrick sighed. "As secure as a cell phone can be."

"Understood. Can you tell me what the situation is?"

"No, sir, not really. Uh, how long would it take you to get out here?"

Craig thought for about one second. There were several hints in Derrick's response. First, calling him sir, besides being annoying, also told him absolutely how serious this was. Derrick was obviously scared shitless. Second, assuming Craig would drop everything and get there ASAP indicated that Derrick was on to something he *knew* would cause Craig to do precisely that.

"Exactly where is *here?*" Craig asked.

"I'm at the port at Benicia, California," Derrick answered.

Craig was puzzled. "And where the hell is that?"

"It's in the Bay Area."

"OK. I'll call you back in five minutes or less."

"I'll be right here, and I hope it's less," a very anxious Derrick replied.

Craig didn't need approvals, nor did he seek them. He jumped in a black CIA Chevrolet Tahoe, popped the light on top and hit the siren. He was at Ballard Air Force Base in less than 11 minutes. Along the way he made two phone calls. He called the chief flight director at Ballard first, requesting an emergency flight to Benicia, California, or the nearest capable airport facility with a helicopter waiting to take him to the Port of Benicia.

"When do you need to go?" the chief flight director asked.

"I am on my way to the base now—ETA T minus nine."

"Shit, you must have some burr under your saddle today, boy," said the captain as he hung up.

Then Craig talked to Derrick. "I'm on my way. I'll be there in under three hours. Here is an operations code. This is my operation now. If anyone gives you any trouble, you tell them exactly that. If they have any questions, refer them to the number on my card, give them the code, and someone will explain the situation to them."

There should have been a third call, but as would happen too often when Craig got into mission mode, he'd forget all about his personal life and how Scott would feel.

Derrick understood, but as he hung up he said out loud, "Yeah, not that they will like the explanation of the situation," air-quoting the word *situation*. His fear, and justifiably so, was the shit storm about to fall on him from his director. The FBI hates losing control—and playing second fiddle to the CIA on a domestic case pisses them off like nothing else.

JUNE 25, 16:17 EDT

Flight from Washington, D.C.

The F-16 isn't exactly a comfortable plane. In fact, it's not comfortable at all. And a cross-country journey in one is downright torturous, tempered only slightly by its being damn fast. With in-flight fueling capability, you don't even have to stop, but you must slow down a bit, which is both blessing and curse if you happen to have the world's smallest bladder. Even that has a remedy. It's not elegant, since it involves an absorbable seat pad, but it works.

Craig's 15:44 PDT touchdown at Travis Air Force Base was the best solution, primarily because it's known as the Air Force gateway to the Pacific. No one plane is given any particular notice. Secondly, it's a short twenty miles from the Port Benicia facility. So close that Craig barely had time to call Derrick to let him know he soon would be arriving by helicopter.

Craig was confused about this from the outset. Rarely would he go off on such a priority mission with so little information. One thing he knew for sure, though, the fear in Derrick's voice was unmistakable: the young agent simply had no idea where to turn, whom to trust, or what to do.

From the phone call to shaking Derrick's hand at Amports' facility, a little over 3 hours had passed. From Craig's perspective, that was pretty amazing; from Derrick's point of view, it had been an eternity.

Derrick had spent the past three hours with the bare bones bomb squad of one and their boss, Charlene Thornton, staring at a car that obviously contained a bomb. Preliminary testing confirmed it was emitting radiation waves consistent with nuclear fuel. This information made it easy for Derrick to convince his boss that Craig should be the officer to lead the investigation, and that it was best the CIA took lead from here. Derrick had been filled with self-doubt. Calling Craig instead of following protocol had been a huge risk, but it was already clear to everyone it had been the right call.

On seeing Craig jump out of the Apache tactical helicopter, Derrick felt a huge weight lift. "Thanks for doing this, Craig. I am probably in a heap of trouble." Derrick turned to his boss. "This is Charlene Thornton, Special Agent in charge of the San Francisco division, and the one who's toes I've stomped on by calling you in."

"There's nothing you can do now about decisions you've made. Stick to them. Feel confident you made the right call. Ms. Thornton, it's a pleasure to meet you, and I hope we can work together despite the blatant disregard for protocol," Craig said, intentionally throwing Derrick under the bus, knowing that Derrick knew exactly what he was doing.

"Please, call me Charlene. And I'll be blunt. I'm none too happy, but from what I've seen so far, this is something I'm happy to pass on," then with a smile, added, "Derrick said you were sharp, but my ego is just fine."

"So, are going to tell me what the hell I pretty near killed myself to get here for?" Craig asked.

"I know one thing for sure: we're in way over our heads."

"Come on," Craig said. "Let's take a look."

Walking into the shop, Craig instantly noted the taped-off car. The simple Home Depot–branded orange construction tape and small area it encompassed around allowed him a sigh of relief. He even snorted a chuckle under his breath.

Derrick went around to the other side. Charlene was content to keep her distance. Craig and Derrick both poked their heads into the rear door openings almost simultaneously. Derrick pointed to the cylinder-shaped device and began to tell the story of how it had been discovered.

When Derrick reached for the cylinder, Craig stopped his hand cold, slowly shook his head and mouthed the word *no* as if even talking might set the thing off. He motioned for them both to leave. Once outside, he instructed Derrick to clear the building and seal it up. "Close every door and window, any opening to the outside. Who knows about this?"

"Two technicians and their supervisor, me, the bomb guy, my boss, and you. I don't think the supervisor knows much, to be honest, but both technicians are pretty suspicious."

Craig wasn't too pleased with the already long list. Though, it was clear Charlene had attempted to keep the circle small, hence the lack of FBI tape or full on bomb squad. "OK, they need to be isolated. I want them in isolation at the nearest hospital capable of treating radiation poisoning ASAP. Use the military chopper and keep it quiet. Maybe the VA is the best bet. Use the ops code I gave you. Admit them there as prisoners."

Derrick was shocked. "Prisoners!"

"Yes, there doesn't need to be a charge with that code, but they won't be able to leave or speak to anyone or have any visitors and they will be under twenty-four-by-seven guard."

The still-shocked Derrick just shook his head, saying, "Shit! The bomb guy too? Don't we need him?"

"If this is what I think it is—and what he thinks it is—it's way beyond his training to deal with, which is why I barely acknowledged him and why he's basically been standing around, in case you hadn't noticed," Craig told him. "Next, we need to scan this place for radiation and see what exposure there's been. Get the Department of Energy here ten minutes ago, and again make sure they understand they are to keep it quiet."

"Whoa, wait just a fucking minute! What do you mean radiation poisoning and radiation exposure? I've been around that thing for almost four hours now," Derrick quavered.

"You've been taking your iodine?"

"Yeah, but that's a crock and you know it!"

"No, it's not. It'll help, and once we know what we're dealing with, we'll get you off to the hospital, too."

"As a prisoner?" Derrick feverishly wondered.

Craig ignored the comment and told him, "We've also got to get something to eat."

"You've got to be kidding. How can you be thinking of food?"

"We'll need our energy. We've got to keep our strength up. Weak and irritable will lead to irrational mistakes and faulty decision making. I'm being pragmatic."

Derrick wanted to scream out but thought better of it. Keep a cool head, he told himself, and with some luck or the help of a guardian angel you might just survive.

Craig could see Derrick's mental wheels turning. "Your blood sugar is already low. Your remark about being a prisoner demonstrated that, so you can see now how critical food is?"

At once Derrick recognized that here was a man who knew how to survive, knew how to plan and strategize every component, and implement the processes necessary to succeed. Derrick would never doubt him again.

JUNE 25, 16:33 PDT

Benicia, California

One chopper was leaving the port just as another was coming in. To Craig, clearly this was going to attract unwanted attention. While most of the day shift had already left, Craig still asked to see the manager of the facility, who turned out to be the vice president of Amports' Benicia operations, Mark Templin, requesting that the port be shut down entirely.

"Only security staffs are to remain, and they are to go home as soon as we are able to secure the facility ourselves. Any incoming ships are to be instructed to hold at sea."

The radiation team was offloading from the chopper and suiting up as Craig wrapped up his discussion with the manager, who was obviously irate.

"Closing down the port and sending everyone home is difficult enough, but not knowing why makes it a very tough nut to swallow." Yet when he saw the radiation team in full gear, he abruptly changed his tune. "Give me twenty minutes. When can my security people be relieved as well?" asked a now very cooperative Mr. Templin.

"Our security personnel will need to come by road, so we need an hour to get this place under wraps. Also, Mr. Templin, I need you and everyone working here to understand one thing very, very clearly: no one says anything to anyone about what's going on here! There was a gas leak and it's being taken care of. Are we clear?"

Templin knew the tone. It said, *you fuck with me and you'll likely never see the light of day again*; so he said while nodding, "Yeah, yeah. It's crystal . . . clear."

He took one more look at the radiation team setting up, then jogged back to his office. Once he heard the words *national security*, Templin knew this was not a battle he wanted anything to do with.

The radiation measurements began fifteen yards from the building's entrance. Once they were determined to be safe, another test was done at ten yards and so on until the team was at the entrance. Then they sent in a remote, a radio frequency–operated vehicle that cost thousands more than the sensor equipment it was carrying.

Once inside, the RF vehicle continued the five-yard-at-a-time approach, gaining on the little Chevy cautiously, as so far none of the tests produced any results of dangerous radiation. There were, however, low levels of radiation from the very first test. Inside the building, the levels became stronger and increased in intensity until the remote was right next the contaminated Chevrolet.

Since the indications of radiation were still at low levels, the team decided they could approach—wearing their suits—with more sophisticated equipment for a closer look.

If ever there were a time when Craig would like to be proven wrong, that time would be now. That they were dealing with an exceptionally well made and shielded nuclear device was something he could have gone his entire career being wrong about.

JUNE 25, 17:33 PDT

Benicia, California

"**N**o offense, but you were right. You're in way over your head," Craig muttered.

Derrick nodded. "Yeah, now what? How do we keep a lid on this? Is that even what we do?"

"Yeah, let's start there. Get this contained. Restrict the airspace. No boats are to approach and close the roads in here."

Charlene Thornton was standing beside Derrick when Craig informed her Derrick would report to him directly but didn't raise the slightest objection.

Derrick laughed. "I feel like I've been requisitioned like a Humvee or something."

After just an hour, the entire Amports facility was swamped with spooks and military personnel. Benicia is a facility given to being locked down. It started out as a ship building operation that went into full swing during World War II.

Like all such facilities, access from public roads was limited. The biggest trick was to discreetly clear out the last of the Amports employees in such a way they wouldn't appear suspicious.

The gas leak excuse would work to get people out, but once things got crazy with more and more military personnel and Humvee's all over the place, there'd have to be another excuse. Templin suggested they cite incidents of sabotage and mild fights recently over a labor dispute.

It worked like a dream. The employees were so pissed that they'd been locked out by federal marshals, they never noticed all the unusual activity and just left, off to a nearby watering hole to discuss their retaliation fantasies.

Once that was taken care of, the more sensitive measure of having the management and security staff handled was required. They naturally couldn't have a civilian out in public with any knowledge of what was going on at the port that involved the D.O.E. So they were "arrested," and once it was impressed on them that they would be back in confinement in short order if they said a word, they were released.

Department of Energy is called in when anything atomic in nature needs to be assessed. When the military or intelligence agencies are involved, it's always a tenuous involvement. The D.O.E. has the data records and testing capabilities to not only identify the purity and potential destructive power of a nuclear device but also determine precisely what reactor enrichment facility it came from.

D.O.E.'s immediate job was to assess the radioactive shielding of the atomic material inside the device. To those who already had been exposed to the device, this was the question they most needed answered.

Nancy Martins, PhD, was flown in from the D.O.E. facility in Nevada. She hated to fly, and she especially didn't trust helicopters. It was her opinion those things obviously were cheating the laws of physics.

Craig wanted everything and everyone to go through him. There needed to be one line of communication and command, and until someone higher up showed up to relieve him, that's how it was going to run. Martins immediately had an issue with this.

"I'm glad you are here, ma'am. Name's Craig Stout, CIA. Can you assemble your team and equipment as soon as possible? The device is in that building. Where do you want to set up in relation to the location?"

"Craig Stout, CIA, huh? Who the hell made you God?"

"Not God, ma'am. This is a national security crisis that appears to have been launched from a foreign source, making it the purview of the CIA. Being the ranking CIA operative here, I'll be in charge until one of three people tell me otherwise."

"What three people?"

"CIA Director Richards, Department of Homeland Security Secretary Bonner, or the president of the United States. Are we clear, ma'am?"

"Fine, let's get our jobs done," said Martins. She realized this wasn't an ego trip Craig was on and that he was plainly doing his job. He was being very direct about it, which was something she not only appreciated but respected. "But call me ma'am one more time and I'll turn you into one. Are we clear on that? Nancy will be fine."

Craig grinned. "Sure thing, Nancy. I hope we can prevent a disaster here, and you'll be instrumental in that."

"I'd like to set up ten meters from the building. A canopy is all I want. No walls, nothing to contain anything, as much free-flowing ventilation as possible. Not that that will do much, but it won't make things worse by containing radiation in a small area."

"We'll set that up while your team is setting up their equipment. I assume your power needs will be substantial?

"Not terribly, but reliability is critical. We can't have circuits blowing in the middle of an analysis."

JUNE 26, 13:10 KDT

Changwon, South Korea

There's very little more intimidating than an army of official-looking men in black suits descending upon your plant in the middle of the day asking to see the plant manager. Mr. Jong-Dong Park, production manager of the GM Daewoo plant, while annoyed, wasted no time getting to the conference room where his assistant had assembled the legion of bureaucrats. Mr. Seung-Gyu Kim could have gone alone. He'd be the only one talking, but this show of force was intended to prevent anyone from being coy or not providing all the information and assistance he could.

Kim got to the point, directly and brashly. "I need to know about the shipment of cars that arrived in Benicia, California, on June 21. Leave nothing out. Include anything you might remember, even if it seems completely irrelevant. Please leave it to me to determine what may or may not be important."

Something about being at war with its northern neighbor for more than a half century had made South Korea's governmental security agencies some of the best and probably most paranoid in the world, rivaling only Israel when it came to the latter.

Kim had achieved his position as director of South Korea's National Intelligence Service (NIS) by being particularly paranoid and determined. He apparently had no sense of humor. He was all business all the time. He chose to show up at the GM-Daewoo Technology plant in person for one reason exclusively: to scare the hell out of them.

The call to his office three hours earlier, on a secure line from U.S. Secretary of Homeland Security, Michael Bonner, was put through by the operations director immediately upon hearing the code indicating the call was not routine. "Mr. Kim, we have a critical situation. Actually, to be blunter, we are in the midst of a national crisis, the scope of which is something potentially even beyond our worst-case scenario. Do I have your full attention?"

Kim coolly responded, "Tell me."

"This morning we investigated what at first glance appeared to be a low-grade bomb hoax at the port processing facility in Benicia, California. A car built by GM-Daewoo Technical in Changwon was set aside due to a manufacturing defect. During the repair process, a bomb was discovered in the vehicle's fuel tank. As it turns out, it is no hoax at all. At this moment, we are still determining the capabilities of the weapon. Of one thing we are certain, though, it is atomic." There was silence on the other end of the line. "Mr. Kim are you still there?"

Kim didn't miss a beat. "Of course. I am just trying to assess what I can do for you. I seriously doubt such a device would have been installed at the factory."

"I doubt that as well, but we do know it came with the car from Korea," Bonner said, with no attempt to disguise the chastising tone. "I have a team on their way to Seoul. Their ETA is nine hours from now. In the meantime, what I need from you is a complete background of where the car was built, where it went from the factory, how it got to the shipping yard, when it got on the ship, who drove it on the ship, et cetera. I want to know everything about this car down to the serial numbers for the rolls of steel the damn thing was stamped from. In fact, if someone farted in the seat of that car, I want to know about it! Can I count on your cooperation?"

Kim was, of course, pissed about his American counterpart treating him as a subordinate, but he didn't take it personally. He knew the guy was just an arrogant prick. He was pretty sure Bonner knew he couldn't stand him. It was something about the tone he used with Bonner.

Kim was right. Bonner kept his fingers on the receiver after placing it in the cradle. He felt something about the conversation wasn't quite right. He was literally trying to put his fingers on it.

On Kim's side of the world, in his own office, he too pondered the phone, but his suspicions were hardly newfound; he'd never trusted the American. He'd always felt that Bonner was hiding something, and not in the sense of a man playing his cards close to his vest. His was a more sinister element of deception.

The plant manager of the GM-Daewoo Changwon plant hosted this illustrious group that afternoon without any knowledge of the situation on the other side of the Pacific. Park could think of a million things he'd rather be doing—tooth extraction without anesthetic even sounded better. As to fearing them, South Korea's National Intelligence Service may not be as notorious as Russia's FSB, but still, not a meeting anyone in his right mind looks forward to.

Kim handed the manager a slip of paper on which was written *Chevrolet Spark, Red, 4-Door, VIN number KL1CD66A6KC107426.*

"I need to know everything about this car. What day it was built, using what components, supplied by what suppliers, when those parts arrived, how they arrived, how it was transported to the shipyard, when it was loaded on the ship, who drove it, and so on. Like I said before, leave nothing out. You and your team have one hour. I will wait here."

Park wasn't able to move. He was stunned, and clearly the nation's top spy now before him didn't have a clue about the complexity of what he was asking. Park swallowed hard and walked out of the room, dreading his eventual return in an hour, as he knew he would be bearing less information than he'd been asked to gather. It was impossible to access that much information in the time allowed. With the VIN number, the build data was a simple matter of a computer inquiry; but the rest of it would take time, and he mumbled out loud, "God knows if they keep names of the drivers for each car, but it's doubtful."

JUNE 26, 14:47 KDT

Changwon, South Korea

When Park reluctantly entered the conference room, he'd received no fewer than four notifications of information coming from the staff at the plant, but it would not be within the hour time limit allotted. After one hour and thirty-seven minutes, the chief spy had had enough. "My patience has been exhausted, Mr. Park. What do you know?"

"What you have asked of us is not something we typically have records for, sir. While the build data information is relatively easy, and all those documents have been turned over to you, the questions about people involved in the process are not as easy to track down."

He handed over a complete itemized report of every component in the car of question. He listed each part by name, part number, supplier, supplier plant identity, ship date, ship method, container number, even the precise time that component was installed during assembly, and the employees at the assembly station at that time. It was an exhaustive level of detail that would not provide any tangible leads. There would be no anomaly associated with the assembly process or any aspect of the supplier chain. Just-in-time parts delivery ensured all this data was accurate; each part has a barcode that is scanned and delivered to the assembly line at the precise location just as the specific car it is intended for also arrives at that location.

Kim glanced through the report, but saw nothing that stood out, nothing to question. He asked the plant manager if there was anything to this information that would be unique to this particular car.

"No, sir, nothing. Everything about the build of this car is standard. There were no delays on the line, and no one stopped the line for any reason, which is something every associate is encouraged to do when they suspect the slightest problem. I am totally confident that there was nothing unusual about this car."

A visibly frustrated and growling Kim frowned and dropped the papers on the overly polished table. "I hate to tell you this, but something is very unusual about this car—so unusual that I am here. So damn unique that it has top intelligence agencies scrambling agents from all over the globe to our country at this very moment. You *will* find *something* for me to tell them before they arrive."

Kim was keenly aware that the problem with using fear as a motivator is that when used even subtly, the result it produces might not be based on truth. The answers received may be a convenient and expedient way to remove the threat of reprisal from the information gatherer. It is for these reasons that coerced confessions were not acceptable in a society where justice is the goal of prosecution. Coercion wasn't discarded as a tool due to some moral objection about mistreatment of the accused; it was discarded because it produces unreliable results counterproductive to the goal.

Consequently, when another thirty-two minutes had passed and Park had given his report of the movements of the car as it exited the assembly plant, Kim should have realized his pressure for answers could backfire.

"The car was staged in our yards for about nineteen hours, at which time it was loaded on truck number fifteen thirty-four at thirteen twenty-five for transportation to the Port of Busan, where it waited for another twenty-two hours before being driven onto the ship *Trinidad*. The personnel records indicate that Jong-Kip Chung was driving truck number fifteen thirty-four that day. He has been requested to report here. There was nothing associated with the transportation of the vehicle that would appear to be anything other than ordinary."

Kim's poker face revealed nothing of his thoughts.

"How long does it take a truck to get from here to the port?"

"It takes between fifty-five and one hundred twenty minutes depending on traffic, sir."

"And how long did it take this truck?"

"We don't know, sir. That isn't logged." Sweat beads on his upper lip showed how nervous Park was in even trying to explain the process. Kim was intimidating even when he wasn't trying to be.

"Wouldn't it be part of the security measures of the port to know exactly what is arriving and when it arrives?"

"Perhaps, sir, but we don't run the port and have no authority to request their records."

"But you know when the car was loaded on the ship by the port workers?"

"Yes," Park began to explain, his face pained with discomfort. "Those records are provided to us routinely as a customer. The vehicle's barcode is scanned as it passes over the entry ramp of the ship, and the data is electronically transmitted to us with every outbound ship. It's an automated process."

"But you don't know when the cars are driven off the truck?"

"No, there is no process in place to scan the barcode at that point. I don't know how, from a distribution point of view, we would find that data of value. Each truck comes in at different times and unloading depends on the convenience of the longshoremen. They are, as you know, sir, members of a very strong union and only work within the agreed-on guidelines."

As is customary in Korean culture, Park answered the questions as directly as they were asked.

With this information, Kim stood up from the table, and of course, everyone followed his lead. He requested that only his second in command join him. Kim pulled his most trusted deputy aside: he was to go to the Port of Busan to get the entry information for the date in question. Every truck would be logged. Finding out when this truck showed up to be off-loaded was critical to establishing a timeline.

Walking back to the conference room, Kim had a feeling he was getting somewhere. Progress was being made, and at least there was a visible trail, finally. Something bothered him still about Park's answers about the transportation. *There was nothing associated with the transportation of the vehicle that would appear to be anything other than ordinary,* he'd said—almost as if he'd tried to make it appear to be a dead end. And as the questions he asked Park showed, there were plenty of holes in the process about which he had no information. Those holes established that he couldn't definitively know one way or the other if the transportation process had been ordinary or not. Kim realized he'd pushed him hard but didn't think the intelligence was compromised. The comment was probably nothing more than Park wanting to be done with the whole affair; he did have a plant to run, after all.

The conference room was still full, still tense, with a weight to the air that was stifling. Kim well knew he was responsible for that and took a certain pride in it.

"Mr. Park, can you tell me when your truck driver will be here?"

"Sir, he is due at the port with a load of cars, waiting to be off-loaded. He should be back here in three hours at the most."

The tension finally got the most of South Korea's chief spy. He exploded. "What the hell do you mean he's waiting to off-load?! I was very certain I'd impressed upon you the importance of my being here. For fuck sake my simply being here should have impressed that upon you! He is to proceed directly here, right now, no waiting, by the fastest means possible! Am I making myself perfectly clear?"

Looking like he'd just been whacked with a stick, Park said he'd send a car to retrieve the truck driver.

Little could Park have known, but Jong-Kip Chung was not at the Port of Busan. He was at that moment on an Asiana flight bound for Beijing that had left almost forty-five minutes earlier from the Busan airport. The truckload of Chevrolets had been abandoned three miles from the airport. The truck driver—having been tipped off by a Daewoo executive willing to betray his country for a handsome sum—had flagged down a car on its way into the airport and asked to be dropped off at the terminal.

"I'll just call my boss and wait for them to arrive there," Chung told his lift, and continued to explain, "my cell phone is dead." In fact, his phone was lying at the bottom of the Yellow River so it couldn't be used to track him.

JUNE 26, 15:22 KDT

Busan, South Korea

The driver knew this part of the plan was very specific: if anyone asked about him, *he was to leave the country as fast as possible.* He executed his exit plan carefully. This was certainly no ordinary truck driver. In fact, Chung was one of North Korea's MSS intelligence assets.

The flights from Busan to Beijing always had one to three seats booked on them by the agency that were canceled methodically between one to two hours before the scheduled departure. This insured availability on every flight departing the country for MSS Agent Jong-Kip Chung to walk up last minute and get a seat immediately.

Beijing was a strategic destination. While there were few flights a week between Beijing and Pyongyang, North Korea, they were the only commercial flights into the isolated regime. Chung's getaway was now as dependent on luck as strategy. Would he arrive in Beijing in reasonably close proximity to when the next flight departed to Pyongyang? Would he have to depend on the streets of Beijing for cover for hours or even a day? How long would it be before South Korea or America was able to secure the cooperation of the Chinese government in issuing a lookout for one Jong-Kip Chung with photos and a description? He knew he had hours, but a day or more would exponentially decrease his odds of escape.

When he felt the plane's wheels leave the tarmac of Busan, he relaxed, but not without reservation. Planes can be turned around, and in a case such as this, would most likely be escorted to a secure landing strip by fighter jets. No, Jong-Kip would not relax fully until he was safely in Pyongyang. That was something he felt pretty good about as well, since it was 15:35 on Wednesday; the next flight to North Korea from Beijing was scheduled for Thursday at 10 A.M. He would use a North Korean passport issued under the name of Robert Lee. Who says the North Koreans have no sense of irony?

Even so, his photo was taken at least three times at Busan Airport. It would be a matter of hours before his destination was known. He could only hope there was time enough for the plane to land and the passengers to disembark before Chinese authorities began looking for him.

Chung's North Korean passport indicated he was an electrical engineer. His cover, supported by official documents, was that he would be visiting three firms in China that were looking to provide North Korea with technology, parts, and machinery to update that nation's badly outdated electrical generation and distribution capabilities.

JUNE 26, 16:05 KDT

Changwon, South Korea

"How a truck driver can go missing in the middle of his shift is only a mystery if you believe he actually is just a truck driver," Kim patiently explained to plant manager Park as he shook his hand to say good-bye.

While his team would continue the interviews, and those interviews would begin anew once the American intelligence ops arrived, Kim left the manufacturing complex and headed to Busan's International Airport on a hunch. He almost felt sorry for these people, knowing they would be repeating the same story over and over, some of them for the next several days.

Kim took with him the personnel file of this Chung character, knowing full well that he would not be traveling under that name, but the photo from his company ID card would be most useful.

JUNE 26, 16:55 KDT

Busan, South Korea

When Kim arrived at the airport, he walked through the entrance for Korean Airlines and strolled past the tidy check-in counters and on to the dozen or so immigration counters spanning a wide area. A smaller airport, Busan was pretty easy to get into and through quite fast.

Of course, Kim needed only to show his badge and ID card and he was discreetly waved through. The security office was upstairs and down a quiet hallway, directly over the immigration agents' desks.

Kim walked into the security office, where he found a very nicely dressed young woman sitting behind a waist-high counter. She stood and smiled, and asked in a quiet and demure voice, "May I assist you?"

He showed her his badge and ID, and without sounding arrogant or pushy, told her in a voice that ensured there'd be no arguing, "I know the way to the director's office. I'll show myself." She bowed and sat back down.

When Kim entered the director's office, he was surprised to see two uniformed airport security officers seated with their feet on the director's desk. *How appalling,* he thought, *that one of them is even sitting in the director's chair.* He politely asked to see the man in charge. This being Korea, it was safe to assume the director wasn't a woman.

The somewhat lackadaisical guard in the director's chair asked with a lazy drawl, "Who wants to know?" with an attitude completely unacceptable in Korean culture. Kim could not have been just anyone, and it was highly unlikely that a simple passenger, confused and lost, could've gotten by the receptionist. And besides, given his dress and age, the comment was a serious insult.

With bigger axes to grind, Kim decided to let this cocky prick stew in his own juices. He gently placed his National Security Agency identification, open with the shiny brass shield proclaiming DIRECTOR in both Roman and Korean characters, on the desk in front of the insubordinate.

The change in attitude was almost humorous to watch. The guy was practically stumbling over himself in an attempt to simultaneously look busy and important and yet also be apologetic for his attitude, knowing full well there was no erasing the past two minutes.

"Sir, I'm sorry. Please sir, take a seat. Can I have coffee or tea brought for you?"

"No, just the director of airport security, and as quickly as possible!"

"Yes, sir. Please be comfortable. I'll find him personally and bring him here."

He did just that, returning no more than three minutes later with the boss in tow, his skin glistening with a sheen of nervous sweat.

JUNE 26, 17:22 KDT

Busan, South Korea

The director of security operations at Busan Airport has no easy job, but it's nothing like Incheon or LAX, for example. You find comfort in small things when your job is a powder keg of stress—where you must balance security with the demands of free trade geopolitics and civil liberties.

Michael Choi was not that flustered. Many officials from police and security services had shown up to expedite an agent with a, prisoner, deportee or person of interest through customs and security; but the director of the NSA in person? That made his butt cheeks clench like a schoolboy being called to the principal's office.

"Mr. Choi, we need a private place to talk."

Immediately, Choi motioned for the others in the room to leave.

"Sir, is there someone coming through customs, or is there something else I can do?"

"First of all, Mr. Choi, you are never to discuss anything about this day with anyone. Am I clear?"

"Perfectly clear, sir," Choi responded, with quiet respect.

"What are the face recognition capabilities of your software?"

"I doubt it's what you are used to, sir, but it's very good."

"Here is a picture. I need to find out if he was here, and if so, where he was going and under what name he was traveling."

"And you need this right now?"

"I wouldn't be here otherwise," Kim said.

"Yes, yes, of course. It was a stupid question, sir."

Kim's lack of response was its own acknowledgment that he agreed.

JUNE 26, 17:47 KDT

Busan, South Korea

Choi carefully placed the picture on the scanner. Once the image was in the system, it automatically searched all still pictures taken that day at the passport control processing desks. This was the best place to look first, as everyone going through has a clear full-face picture taken as they are being questioned by the immigrations officer.

When people complain about having to remove their sunglasses, reading glasses, head scarf or hat at the window, they have no idea the request is made so the picture can be taken without obstruction.

The machine buzzed and occasionally clicked as the photos flashed through its hard drive and memory. A few minutes later, the flashing photos stopped and the photo it stopped on was linked to a passenger who came through desk 17. There was a scan of the passport as well, showing the name of Mr. Chung.

Kim was surprised but not shocked the information came up so quickly—as promised, of course; but promises from government contractors aren't any better than those from civilians. He knew this was the last they would see of that name or passport.

"Do you scan the boarding card as well?" questioned Kim.

"Afraid not, sir. We're less concerned about the destination than we are about the identification, citizenship, visitor status, watch list status, and primary national security protocols."

Even superspies have "duh" moments. Kim tried to let this go unnoticed. "Your database cross-references with the airlines' databases?"

"Yes, but it isn't in real time, sir."

"I see. And when will we be able to see the airlines' data and manifest lists?"

"We get their data automatically at one minute after midnight every night—but I'm guessing that's not going to be fast enough?"

"Good guess. What are our other options?"

JUNE 26, 18:08 KDT

Busan, South Korea

In one of the most paper-wasting exercises in the modern world of business, a manifest is printed on continuous form paper for every flight. It contains the name of every passenger and that person's assigned seat number, frequent flyer status, the number of bags each passenger checked, details of any connecting flights and many other details such as flight crew, the weights and balances of the aircraft, and other messages from the airline, maintenance, and air traffic control, among others.

The dilemma for Kim was that the printout is printed from the gate desk and handed over to the lead flight attendant, who distributes the information needed by the flight crew, and then posts first class and business class passenger information for the attendants working those cabins.

"You mean it's on the plane?" Kim asked the security director, to make sure he understood what had just been explained.

"Yes, sir, it is, but we can get duplicate copies from the gate for any flight that has left that gate within the past six hours. But we'll need manpower, unless you have an idea of what flights we should check first."

Kim smiled. He knew the destination.

"We need the manifests for all flights to Beijing."

JUNE 26, 16:05 CDT

Beijing, China

Chung's flight to Beijing took off without much drama, but he still didn't relax. While his training had provided the discipline and confidence necessary to appear calm even when all his instincts told him not to, his instincts had taken over and betrayed him. For seven long years he'd been under cover at the plant in South Korea, completely isolated from any handler or comradeship; keeping his skills honed was difficult in that solitary situation.

On that aircraft, his failure to hide his anxiety became obvious. He was twitchy. His eyes darted around and he started to arouse the suspicion of the flight crew. The flight attendant asked her lead supervisor if she could observe the passenger in seat 5D. The consensus: something was not quite right. Following protocol, they called the flight deck and requested the captain or first mate to come out for a look.

When the captain called in to both the originating airport and arriving airport security control, Mr. Chung—without knowing it—found himself the subject of an investigation by no fewer than three countries.

Upon arrival at Beijing, Chung had several new friends he'd never see, let alone meet. His every step was being observed, every glance and body movement recorded by cameras—and he was being watched by intelligence officers in the arrivals hall.

All passengers arriving in China must clear immigration and customs even if continuing on to another destination, as in the United States. The difference in China is that placing tracking devices into the pages of your passport is not illegal. One such chip was installed in Chung's passport without his knowledge. His last name was now Lee and he was traveling as a citizen of the Democratic People's Republic of Korea, but thanks to the observant nature of the flight crew, his new name would be known to those in South Korea and in the United States.

Any detective will admit that all too often the success of an investigation is based on pure luck. Such was the case this time. As Chung/Lee left the terminal, the tracking beacon activated in his passport—and the Chinese authorities were not worried about him ditching it. They knew he would have to use the same passport to leave China.

JUNE 26, 19:05 KDT

Seoul, South Korea

Kim commissioned a military plane to take him back to Seoul so he could conduct the rest of this investigation from his office. He knew his target would be headed to Pyongyang, North Korea. He also knew how few flights entered the capital city of North Korea and that all those flights originated in Beijing; and more importantly, he knew when that next flight was scheduled. Now to get an agent on that flight!

Since an agent from South Korea would be next to impossible, Kim thought his only chance would be to get an agent from China on the flight, knowing full well he wouldn't be able to trust him at all. Worse, it meant he'd owe one hell of a favor to the Chinese security agency, a group he'd much rather not owe.

He'd have to weigh the risks. Getting the Chinese to cooperate meant a certain quid pro quo. Yet, knowing they were allies of the North, he wasn't at all sure anything he obtained from them would be of value. In fact, the Chinese could make things even worse.

He pondered his position and decided to call that asshole in Washington, D.C. If anyone was to be in debt to the Chinese, he'd prefer that it be Michael Bonner.

Bonner's reading of Kim couldn't be more off base. Kim was dedicated to his profession and his ethics were unimpeachable. What Bonner was picking up on and misreading as suspicious, though, was actually disdain. Kim couldn't stand the man and wouldn't be surprised to learn if Bonner were in fact behind this whole affair.

Kim's call to the American would go as follows: give facts, ask for direction on the next steps the American would like to take, and exchange no pleasantries. His wife would tell him he could fake it if he didn't like someone; she'd say *just pretend*, but for

Kim it wasn't possible. He'd work with the man but had no intention of pretending to like it.

Bonner agreed to ask the Chinese to put an agent on the flight solely to watch and monitor. He'd also let Kim know what was happening next, though this assurance provided Kim little solace. Rather, he wondered if asking Bonner had even been a good idea.

Kim wanted to grab Chung in Beijing, drug him, threaten him with death, and if that failed, threaten him more directly between his legs. That never failed. Even illiterate gangs knew it was always more effective, more so even than waterboarding.

Bonner wanted to make sure this guy was indeed working for the North, see where he led them, and then decide how best to handle it.

That strategy seemed not only ill-advised to Kim but downright stupid and reckless. Assuming Bonner did finally think the North was involved in this, how did he propose to go in to get him at that point?

Once someone is in the North, that person is gone—so much so, he is as good as dead when it comes to being of use for information. Bonner's position made no sense, and Kim now suspected his original instinct and distrust of the man were more than likely spot on.

JUNE 27, 08:00 CDT

Beijing, China

Chung/Lee showed up at Beijing International three hours before his scheduled departure to Pyongyang, as he'd been trained to do: be early, don't risk issues with security, and appear to be like any other passenger. The problem, though, was that this was Chung's first and only mission, and while his training was strong and his dedication to "father" Kim Jong-un fervent, he clearly wasn't willing to die, and his facial expressions and body language once more exposed him.

Kim did manage to get an agent to Beijing as well, and the agent's reports confirmed how big a mistake Bonner was making. Chung's level of fear proved he was no valued asset. Given the nature of this mission, the North would want no loose ends—and Chung was certainly that. Most likely, he would be terminated upon giving his report in Pyongyang.

Kim didn't like it. Chances were this guy didn't know much. He worried Chung was no more than a pawn with instructions to drive a batch of cars to some destination before they were delivered to the port; but that was more than Kim had to go on now. At least maybe he'd know the car's destination, and maybe even find out what had been done to that car and how, and to how many other cars as well.

That thought kept eating at Kim. No one had indicated they even considered the possibility there could be more cars involved. That the Americans found a car—by pure luck—with a nuke quite ingeniously installed in its gas tank was an indication of smoke, not fire. He was certain if they could do this to one car, they could do it to several.

Kim had to get a man on that flight, someone to watch the Chinese watchers: and at any sign of foul play he would intercept Chung. What Kim was about to put into action would either be the end of his career and cause an international incident that would shame South Korea or worse, make China look like a victim of a conspiracy; or, Kim would be 100 percent correct and ensure the salvation of the free world.

Kim had other resources in the American intelligence community. Some were good friends, and it was one such whom he called. The director of the CIA felt much the same way as did Kim about Bonner. In fact, around Washington it was widely believed Bonner fortuitously kept his cabinet position in the new administration as a show of inclusion, an effort to reach out to the other side of the aisle.

Director Steven Richards was an affable if perhaps a dull man. Methodical, slow in his physical mannerisms, of a type at first glance you'd not think to be well suited as director of the CIA. Yet that outward demeanor was a clever cover he created, one he'd carefully crafted along the lines of his favorite TV detective, Columbo. Richards had an intellect that worked at light speed, a mind that captured every detail taken in by his eyes, nose and ears, every sense. Nothing escaped his notice, and best of all, no one involved was any the wiser. He let others do the talking. That way, he could soak in everything around him.

Kim told Richards the entire story up to this point, including his thoughts on the Secretary of Homeland Defense's actions. Kim was well aware he was asking his friend to commit an act of insubordination, one that could also be prosecuted as treason by an ardent government attorney.

Luckily for Kim, Director Richards knew his friend well enough to know just what he was asking. Not only was he sure of Kim's feelings and analysis, he knew that not acting could cause death and destruction on a massive scale. Kim ran through all the red flags from the beginning and described how he felt his skin was being pricked by a thousand needles, that his stomach was being tied up in knots by some sadistic sailor. And that sadistic sailor was Michael Bonner.

JUNE 27, 10:42 CDT

Beijing

The flight in Beijing was prepared for boarding. Everyone's documents had been checked and rechecked. Pyongyang isn't a destination where it's easy to turn around and come back if your papers aren't in order.

As the flight boarded, Chung found his aisle seat in the middle of the cabin. He'd made more of a scene than he'd liked at the gate, insisting on an aisle seat; but it was one thing his training and common logic had taught him: don't trap yourself in an already confined space.

The problem for Chung is that any such request raises suspicions in those customarily dealing with officials of the North Korean regime. Most people on the plane would be nationals of North Korea or Chinese who are as culturally restrained as North Koreans. They simply don't make requests, don't get involved, and if they see something they keep out of it. They live and conduct their every action by a simple adage: *Nails that stick up get hammered down.*

After Chung settled in, he momentarily thought about the extra security screening he'd been subjected to before boarding this flight. He hoped it was just a random selection. The reality was that he'd been tagged for secondary screening long before the boarding process had begun.

The Chinese placed two agents on the flight: one requested by Secretary Bonner, and another that the Chinese routinely placed on this flight. One of these agents was seated across the aisle from Chung, and the other was directly behind him.

Kim had one hell of a time getting an appropriate agent on the flight. His only chance was a Chinese-born Korean in the agency. Getting him to Beijing in time for the flight was also a feat; but in the end, NIS Agent Lim was seated in the center seat right next to the North Korean spy.

Lim was an avid martial arts enthusiast, holding black belts in four different disciplines, and a physical health nut, exhibiting oxlike strength and catlike reflexes. When it came to hand-to-hand combat, he was probably the best agent in about any service. Given the inherent incompatibility of bullets and pressurized fuselages, not relying on a gun had clear advantages; hopefully, the need for his specialty on a commercial flight would be limited.

Lim's inventive strategy was to claim he wasn't feeling well, and that he would appreciate the aisle seat to speed access to the toilet. Chung was visibly shaken. The seat for which he'd fought so hard was about to be lost; but he was disarmed. He simply couldn't deny the ill man his request without arousing more suspicion.

Taking the center seat, he felt as trapped as a rat on a sinking ship. Little did he know he'd just saved his own life.

The request Kim made of Director Richards would make Richards complicit in an illegal mission serious enough to bring down the entire administration. If he was wrong, it would be the end of his political life and there would be no way for him to save face in the shame he would bring to both his country and the United States.

The plan was bold and dangerous. It was fraught with risk and could, in hindsight, end up looking so overreactive, it would make America's trumped-up invasion of Iraq look like an accidental border crossing.

Kim knew that only one agent aboard the flight might not be able to have control for long. If he needed to overpower two or more agents, his chances of saving Chung for questioning were dismally slim.

Kim was convinced that the Chinese agent(s) were under orders from Bonner or the Chinese or the North Koreans to kill Chung rather than risk his interrogation by the South Korean National Security. He was certain beyond any doubt, so much so that every fiber of his body was taut with trepidation. Chung was his sole human lead; his importance could not be overstated.

The United States Air Force provides support for the South Korean Air Force at a base near Seoul. The audacious plan was to scramble six South Korean fighters and six American fighters that would blast into North Korea, engage the commercial flight, and divert it to a landing strip near the northern border of South Korea.

A major highway runs east to west skirting the DMZ precariously close in some places. When driving toward the west, everyone has a curious desire to look to the right, but at the same time not wanting to *appear* to be looking to the right.

At one point, for a distance of nearly four miles on the plateau of a summit, the highway widens from its regular two lanes to a width that would provide ten lanes, with a retractable divider down the middle. A driver along the highway here would notice he or she is suddenly in the middle of what appears to be a massive concrete landscape and may notice lookout towers on the road's south side, but would not know that the depth of the concrete has also increased by nearly two feet.

Before this incident, this national security landing strip had been used for training missions and occasional visits to the DMZ by dignitaries from around the world. Since the distance was more than ninety nautical miles from the expected intercept point in North Korea, it was far more than could be passed off as an accidental border incursion. If discovered, it would most certainly be perceived as an act of war.

The flight commander of the combined force made it crystal clear in his briefing: they were NOT to fire back at any fire they encountered. Under no circumstance were they to fire upon North Korean forces, the hope being they would get in under the North's less-than-sophisticated radar, intercept the plane, and direct it to the landing strip before the North could react.

If the North chose to chase the team out of the country and continued to engage in South Korean airspace, then all bets were off; they were instructed to engage and destroy.

Even the most seasoned pilots knew this would be both a dangerous mission and one that would define the years of their service. This was the mission they would tell their grandkids about.

It was more than ninety miles of sheer terror. Flying with a commercial jet that would slow them down would increase the time it takes to get out of harm's way. They would have to land on an airstrip that doubles as a major highway just south of the DMZ, remove a passenger, and fly him in a fighter jet to U.S. Special Operations Command Korea (SOCKOR). No part of this mission was expected to be easy.

Their best defense was the element of surprise. It would prevent the North from quickly scrambling their fighters, a low flight altitude, and the hope that the North wouldn't fire on a commercial jet—a hope to which no one ever had given much credence. Most everyone believed the North would have no qualms about firing on a commercial plane. All in all, that's a hell of a lot to go wrong. The chance of success was less than twenty percent, not generally considered a valid risk for a military operation.

JUNE 27, 10:52 CDT

Beijing

Agent Lim convincingly faked his illness and left in a dash for the rear toilet as the plane was almost finished boarding. One of the most experienced and talented agents in the South Korean service, Lim was essentially invisible to all aboard the plane. No one had even given the sick man a second look.

Lim immediately identified his Chinese counterparts and was very glad to see just two agents; but he couldn't discount the possibility that the North Koreans well may have installed trained military agents in the cockpit crew. With regard to all details and associated risks, that possibility was the primary threat to the success of the operation.

While in the tiny toilet in the rear of the craft, Lim injected himself with a countermeasure that would protect him from being put down by nearly any known tranquilizer or muscle paralyzing agent—precisely what he would use were he planning to take out someone on a flight.

Lim also prepared another shot for his "prize," as Chung would be referred to in this operation. He quickly returned to his seat. He watched the two Chinese agents making visual signs to each other. This was going to go down quickly. He suspected they would make their move very soon after takeoff, during the climb up to cruising altitude.

He sat slowly, continuing his weak and nauseous act. He quickly analyzed what motions the two men would have to make from their seats to reach his prize; then he ran through the most effective countermeasures in this head. As the plane began to push back from the Jetway, Lim's level of alertness was so keen he could almost see behind him.

The taxi out to the runway seemed to take forever. Lim was beginning to wonder if they were planning to *drive* this jet to North Korea. At last, at the end of the runway, they sat and waited for the tower to clear them for takeoff. The engines wound up while the aircraft was held back by the brakes. This pilot clearly was military trained but hopefully not still in the services of government.

Once the massive brake calipers let loose of the disks, the jet began to thrust forward, increasing speed faster and faster till the nose of the plane lifted off the ground. Seconds later, the landing gear pulled up into the belly of the machine with a loud thump, then a grinding sound as the doors closed, followed by a hush as the airflow under the thin skin of the jet smoothed.

JUNE 27, 11:24 CDT

Chinese Airspace

*A*ny moment now, Lim thought as he pretended to rest in his seat, with his eyes seemingly closed. Then suddenly, the agent behind him moved first, followed almost instantly by the one on his right across the aisle. Lim shot up, twisting his torso and thrusting his arms forward with such speed and force neither man saw the crushing blow to their throats coming. They both dropped. One agent was on his knees then fell over, prone in the aisle, gasping for a breath that would never come. The other agent, directly behind Lim, fell straight back into his seat with the same gasping croak issuing from his crushed larynx, his eyes wide, as though somehow trying to take in what just happened.

Lim saw his prize move, fearing for his life. When he pushed him back down in his seat and pulled his South Korean National Security identification, he instructed the prize in clear clipped words, "Look at it and if you want to live, you will do exactly as you are told."

Chung sat back and nodded in quick agreement. Lim jabbed the needle into his thigh and pressed the plunger in one fluid motion. Instantly, Chung relaxed. The drug was designed to induce compliance without knocking the victim out. The injection included other drugs to make a person alert and to counteract most known suicide drugs Chung might be inclined to use, and, too, drugs that would begin to treat his recent radiation exposure.

Lim dragged the now-dead Chinese agents to the last row of the plane, attracting the attention of an otherwise oblivious flight crew. Limited to one attendant in the rear and one in the front, this airline wasn't known for its adherence to safety or service policies expected in most of the world.

The two attendants rushed Lim as he was pulling the first dead agent to the back. Lim flashed the ID again, and the color left their faces. Both were North Korean, and he was someone they least wanted to tangle with. The fear instilled in North Koreans of the National Security (even if they are from the South) is even more ingrained than that felt by old Russians of their own KGB.

He ordered them to sit in the seats where he would have put the now dead agents or meet a similar fate. Using plastic zip ties, he tightly bound both flight attendants to the arms of the seats and their feet to the aluminum bar underneath, fully immobilizing them.

None of the other passengers on the typically empty flight offered any resistance, content to maintain complete lack of eye contact with Lim or dare make any move at all. They were trying hard to appear invisible, lest they draw the slightest attention.

Returning to his prize, Lim removed the SAT phone from his briefcase and signaled his counterparts in Seoul that the aircraft had been secured, setting phase two into action. Now, to find out if the pilot or first officer were trained agents.

JUNE 27, 12:02 KDT

North Korean Airspace

Several pings were heard over the speakers, indicating the cockpit crew was trying to reach the cabin crew. Usually, four pings is the signal for the cabin crew to pick up the phone to open the communication with the cockpit. Lim knew he better answer but feared there was probably some code the cockpit needed to verify it wasn't a hijacker or terrorist. The crew members would resist if asked for the code, and the delay alone would alert the cockpit to trouble. He picked up the receiver and hoped for the best, and indeed, the first question was to confirm the code. *Fuck!*

At once, the plane dove hard, so hard his head hit the ceiling. Fortunately, the hit was only hard enough to piss him off and not knock him out. Those who were not belted in were flying about the cabin like loose crash test dummies.

The passengers had, till now, maintained their characteristic behavior of keeping quiet no matter what they saw. Lim and his colleagues had counted on it. People who have long lived under a totalitarian regime usually can be counted on to keep their heads down no matter what. Even so, the passengers began to scream hysterically, even as they tightened their belts. Then these famous agnostics spontaneously broke out in prayers—no matter to whose God, just anyone who would listen.

A hard turn left, then to the right, as though the pilot were intentionally trying to break the plane apart and kill them all. Lim realized he would have to convince the pilot to cooperate. Getting to the cockpit door was virtually impossible, yet he was thrown hard against it and came crashing through, damn near landing on the flight-deck control console. Then just as suddenly he was tossed back out. He reflexively spread both arms to catch the doorway and pushed back with all his might, and again came crashing forward—this time into the captain—with tremendous force.

As the captain was hit the aircraft made a violent dive, with Lim wedged between him and the controls. Quickly, Lim reached to the captain's ankle, where he hoped to god he'd find the ceramic tactical knife—that, was indeed there—he grabbed the knife, then in one quick and powerful motion, he stabbed the captain in the chest. The first officer, who had been struggling to take over, felt response feedback as soon as the pilot slumped in his east and let go of the controls, indicating he now had control of the aircraft, thank god.

He leveled the jet at 12,000 feet. Looking to the side and seeing the dead captain, the first officer was faced with a complicated decision. North Koreans are taught from infancy that the state comes first, and God is literally the nation's leader, Il Jong Kim.

Your duty in life is to faithfully serve the state. Agent Lim knew all too well how deeply the programming and indoctrination went, but he also could see this particular pilot had a keen desire to live. That was evidenced by the fact his primary focus was to gain control of the aircraft rather than coming to the aid of his captain.

Lim pulled one of the noise-isolating ear cups off the first officer's head and said to him, "You have two choices: either you and everyone on this plane dies; or, you do as you are told, you will never go back home, but you might live and we will do everything we can to reunite you with your family in the South."

North Koreans all have family in the South, whether they know it or not. Most have been living such an isolationist life, they'd never know. Their relatives on the south side of the border, however, do know and have in some cases been seeking contact with their lost Northern family members through two generations.

The first officer had already made his decision. He hadn't spent his life learning to fly and fighting to get ahead in the communist regime, a system he never fully believed in, only to end up dead. No, quite the opposite. On his flights to China and the very few times he was able to lay over on those flights, he learned the communist leaders in his country were liars—flat-out, bald-faced liars—who lied to their "comrades" entirely for the purpose of maintaining control. He had no family, so this was his ticket out. He smiled to Lim and told him he'd have no trouble.

"Good. Now if your countrymen don't shoot us out of the sky, we just might get out of this alive," said Lim. The grimace on the first officer's face spoke for him: there was indeed a very good chance of being shot down.

JUNE 27, 12:22 KDT

North Korean Airspace

Pouring the power on, the first officer dropped the plane to an altitude of 9,000 feet, dangerously low for the mountainous terrain that is the predominant topography of the Korean Peninsula. He maintained his low altitude and continued on course for Pyongyang. He was told to communicate to the tower that they had suffered a power loss due to a brief failure of the aircraft electronics. Altitude was lost, but the redundant systems had kicked in.

"I report we are not, I repeat, we are not making an SOS. We will continue to Pyongyang as scheduled, and request to maintain current altitude. I'd prefer not to gain altitude so we can begin our descent on time." The tower's scratchy and broken response confirmed but refused clearance for approach at the current altitude.

Lim thought the tower was being awfully strategic. Since at this altitude the radar wouldn't be tracking their location well, if at all, he suspected the refusal was because they wanted to know where they were. This was no doubt so they could deploy fighter jets to their location. This was getting more and more nerve-racking by the minute. He had to keep cool and wait it out. The trick in any combat situation is not to let them see you flinch.

Within ten miles of the airport, the control tower made contact, wanting to know if the captain had a visual on the airport yet. "Do you request an emergency landing?"

The pilot quickly responded. "No, I have visual and full control." When in reality, he made no intention of landing, and headed for the southern border as fast as the plane would go.

The tower's response made both their hearts skip a beat. "We should have visual on you by now. From what direction is your approach?" Lim hoped to hell this first officer could act. He was going to have to pull off a performance worthy of an Oscar. "Our heading is two one eight," informed the first officer.

There followed a long pause from the tower; and then, "We do not have visual. We are scrambling jets to get a visual contact."

"Holy fucking shit, now what?" The first officer asked Lim.

Lim shrugged. "We pray our planes get to us before theirs do."

JUNE 27, 12:30 KDT

North Korean Airspace

im used the SAT phone, knowing it couldn't be traced or heard by the communists below. Calling his control agent, he explained the situation. They could not communicate with the intercept team by radio, who in turn were not to attempt communication with the jet. "The ground has ears."

"How will the team signal our exit?"

Control's cryptic response was, "Oh, you'll know."

Just then, twelve fighter jets took up positions around the Air Koryo jet, forming a protective arrow pattern around the commercial airliner. Two of the fighters dropped back so their noses were even with the passenger jet. The lead plane rocked his wings side to side, the unmistakable "follow me" sign. What they couldn't see was two fighters break off and begin doing zigzags behind the aircraft, looking for the promised North Korean fighters.

The first officer didn't even wait for Lim to tell him. Swallowing hard, he purposefully grabbed the engine controls and slid them to full open. Soon the Russian engineers who designed this aircraft would know what the true top speed of a Tupolev Tu-204-300 was.

While he tried not to run down the aisle with the g-force propelling him toward the rear of the plane, Lim went to retrieve the prize, deciding he wanted him in the cockpit. He quickly released Chung and instructed him to move forward. Securing him to the jump seat, Lim noticed the first officer looking nervous.

"What's wrong?" said Lim, feeling the plane shudder.

"This plane is approved for a top cruising speed of five hundred fifty miles per hour. We are now passing six hundred, and the test pilots never took one over six twenty."

Lim thought the best way to handle the man's fear was to give him bragging rights. "Well, I guess you're Tupolev's new unofficial test pilot." The still fearful yet now more confident first officer cracked a half-smile.

Oddly, Lim wasn't worried about the airplane's flight worthiness. He figured the U.S. military was pretty certain of its absolute limits. No, he was much more worried about being shot down. From Pyongyang to their intended landing strip just south of the DMZ was only ninety air miles; the odds of air-to-air engagement seemed remote. He doubted fighters had been scurried any sooner than the control tower had indicated.

No, that wasn't what he was thinking about right now. Rather, what pressed heavily on his mind was the inescapable fact that the most fortified border on earth is the one between North and South Korea. Getting past it was going to be like running naked through a minefield. The reality of this mission was simple. They could conceivably die within sight of their landing site.

Director Kim sat in his office pale as a ghost, wearing an expression as foreign to him as the feeling that was causing it. That feeling was of complete and utter hopelessness, total wretchedness, the sickness one feels when he accepts the truth of a profound betrayal.

He'd just been briefed by his agent in charge of the North Korea operation. There had been a SAT phone communiqué from the agent he placed aboard the aircraft. Kim was talking to himself, trying to tell himself he saw it coming. *Why the hell am I so shocked? I was suspicious enough to put Lim on the flight in the first place. Still, suspicions are one thing; accepting the realities of those suspicions are another thing entirely.*

The depth of this was impossible to grasp, akin to finding incontrovertible evidence that the most outrageous and audacious conspiracy is true. What earlier could have been dismissed as a slip of the tongue now confirmed, with this new evidence from Lim, that there was a conspiracy—and that the director of U.S. Homeland Security was in on it.

Not trusting Bonner was one thing; not knowing who else was involved were the uncharted waters on which Kim now sailed.

He would decidedly need to play this out—but first he had to call Richards at the CIA. He knew this man soon would be feeling the same racing, rushing emotions.

As he was about to call Richards, Kim's phone rang, the secure line, meaning it was someone who didn't need to go through his assistant. Knowing and fearing who it was, Kim answered, desperate to sound as clipped and detached as always, though seething with anger that was fast becoming a homicidal hatred.

"Director Kim."

"Kim, Director Bonner here. What the fuck's going on? Are you keeping me in the dark on purpose?"

Bouncing around in Kim's mind was the thought, *This asshole is digging in deeper and deeper. He clearly knows his plan failed. Interesting.* Gaining composure now, he would just play it out, as though he had no idea what Bonner was getting at.

"I have nothing to report. The situation was last left with you. We are following our investigative leads at the plant as per your request, but there is nothing new. Last we spoke you were going to arrange eyes on the prize through the Chinese. Wasn't that where we left it?"

On the other end, Bonner felt the air sucked from the room. Realizing Kim was using a tone—*was that victorious elation?*—he knew something was up. His most effective play was to go on the offense.

"Yes," he said tersely, "I've covered that front, but the plane has been intercepted by a team of South Korean and American fighter jets. I want to know on whose fucking authority that has happened. Who sanctioned American fighters to go into North Korea? North, fucking North Korea, for Christ sake!"

"Certainly, sir, only the American military could make such an authorization, and it would seem extremely unprecedented," said an unflappable Kim.

Bonner realized he was being baited. Calmly and delicately he ended the conversation with, "You know where to reach me."

Kim sorely wished that would be the end of it but knew full well the days ahead would be filled with writing reports, making statements, and likely testifying before his leaders about the events that had taken place today. He had set out on this course knowing his career would end either on a note of heroism or in an inferno of a political firestorm. Kim silently accepted he had no other choice.

JUNE 27, 12:36 KDT

North and South Korean Airspace

The Air Koryo jet was pushing limits even Tupolev's engineers hadn't tested for. Full throttle at just 9,000 feet, the jet flashed over the DMZ into South Korea's airspace. The North's ground-to-air missiles sat there, manned but not locked onto the passenger jet. Clearly, they never got a radar lock. Director Kim watched the plane approach from a live video feed from one of the bunkers in the hillside along the highway that was closed to all traffic twenty miles in both directions.

Six South Korean and six American Air Force jets surrounded all positions of the Air Koryo flight, and by now the passengers were convinced they were going to die.

The ground was flashing below them at an alarming speed, from an elevation no one in a passenger jet experiences on an approach for landing. The jet was pushing Mach 0.91, well surpassing the stated cruising speed for which it had been designed. Luckily those passengers couldn't see the MiGs behind them, though from their perspective of being mostly North Korean citizens, the Americans and South Koreans were probably more frightening.

Of course, they had no way of knowing their enemy was now their savior. Those fighter jets were providing a barrier and preventing an attack on the jet. Were they not in place, the passenger jet would have been shot right out of the sky—then proclaimed to be a tragic mishap to the international community. Not that the North gives much of a damn about its image in world politics, but this overkill in defense was positively what kept those passengers alive. That is what Director Kim was counting on: The North simply would be outnumbered; there was no way they could take out the jet *and* every fighter.

As the passenger jet flashed over the DMZ into South Korea's airspace, now came the true test of restraint of North Korea's leaders and, more importantly, of the discipline of the fighters in those jets. Would they stay on their side of the border?

Just to drive home their point, immediately behind the last South Korean fighter, as though orchestrated with months of practice, the surface-to-air flares fired, just to let those North Korean fighters know they were there—and that any move beyond the DMZ would result in their immediately being shot from the sky.

Director Kim, watching the screen, asked the general on the com, "Are you disappointed they are showing restraint?"

Every intelligence service and military organization it supports has inherent animosities; and, too, this was no ordinary general. He was the man responsible for South Korea's domestic defense. He was personally overseeing this mission, and while he was pissed at the spy's implication that he, like most generals, loved war and battle, it gave him pause. To some degree, he *was* disappointed in the response of the North. It showed a level of cowardice he found distasteful.

The general's grunt and sigh were all Kim needed to know he was disappointed in his longtime adversary. Yet, Kim had to wonder, was it cowardice or did the North possibly have other plans in motion? In the life of a spy, every action must be assessed according to its motivation, not merely on the basis of the action itself.

JUNE 27, 12:57 KDT

South Korea, along the DMZ

The passenger jet banked hard back around to line up with the landing strip on the highway below. Since North Korea's only civilian airport facility had no instrumentation for automatically landing planes, the first mate and now captain of the plane had experience with visual-dependent landings. This runway was plenty long, but the elevations were tricky; even with the plane's GPS, it was likely to be a hard touchdown.

The captain pulled back on the throttle, flaps full, gear down, decent control, but not slow. Suddenly, a bang, then the plane bounced up, followed by another thump.

Then the nose gear touched down, the brakes were applied hard, along with the engines' reverse thrusters. The jet, followed down the runway by Humvees with gun turrets, came to a stop as two tanks appeared from the sides and headed toward the front.

The general arrived in a Jeep just as the stairway was being positioned at the jet's door.

General Sung was led up the stairs by two marines in full gear, M16s at their shoulders. One banged the door with the butt of his gun. The door swung open by Agent Lim, who said he didn't think force would be necessary.

It wasn't. The few passengers onboard were sufficiently terrified; not one would even think to do anything stupid. It was enough that they were alive.

Kim's plan was to take five of the passengers into custody and bus the others to Seoul to be flown back to Beijing. He hoped the North Koreans would assume Chung was a random choice on his part, but he knew they'd know who the prize was; the theater was irresistible. From there, he assumed the Chinese would arrest and question the others relentlessly, though he doubted they would be tortured—at least that's what he told himself.

The same could not be promised for the passenger traveling on the North Korean passport under the name of Robert Lee. Oh no, there definitely would be torture in his future.

JUNE 27, 15:39 KDT

USAF Camp Kim, South Korea

"Do you think it was worth the risk and the shit storm that's about to come raining down on us from everyone, including our friends the Americans?" the general groaned to Kim.

"I hope so. I hope with all my being that it was all worth it, and I think it will be, my dear general; after all, the Americans have much bigger things to worry about." Kim knew that Bonner's betrayal would be keeping the American politicians busy for a while.

The old general realized he was out of his league. He could only hazard a guess at what the spymaster might know or think he knew. Either way, he knew an ominous statement when he heard one.

The interrogation room was almost a perfect cliché, only without the bare lightbulb hanging from electrical wiring. Instead the light was provided by wall-mounted fixtures with heavy metal grates surrounding them for protection. No table, no windows. A solid steel slab door banged shut with a metallic clang to make the person feel entombed. A smaller wooden door led to a three-by-three-foot chamber with a stainless-steel toilet and a tiny sink with no hot water.

Chung had no idea how long he'd been there, sitting shirtless in his underwear, allowed toilet breaks and not much else. His "captors" did offer food, but he refused. When he also refused water, an IV was run to keep him hydrated, all part of the plan. Jong-Kip Chung, a.k.a. Robert Lee, was now a guest of the United States Air Force somewhere in the bowels of a building located somewhere within the sovereign territory of the United States of Camp Kim in Seoul, South Korea.

Interrogations such as this follow the usual pattern. Chung had been briefed on what would happen if he were caught. He wasn't a seasoned spy and not trained in techniques to resist and endure interrogation procedures.

It started out this way: food, water, toilet facilities, but with a tinge of humiliation by having you sit around in your skivvies. Strangers come and go, each letting you know in some way you are no longer in control of your life. The removal of a man's freedom, privacy and modesty does things to his psyche. Without the skills to resist, it nullifies him; his confidence abandons him.

Lieutenant Commander John Preston came in much sooner than he would have liked. For a successful interrogation, he preferred to let the suspect stew for a while, wonder about his fate, begin to fear the worst, or at least accept he may never leave. The problem in this case is that there wasn't time. This had to happen much quicker than usual. The kid gloves treatment was over, and things were going to change.

"Let's start with the simple stuff. What's your name?"

"I am Robert Lee."

"Wrong answer, dumb ass! Do you really want to play it this way?"

"I don't understand. I am Robert Lee, a truck driver."

Preston got up and gently and softly walked around behind Chung. He stood there, knowing Chung felt his presence behind him, knowing it intimidated him. He paused for full effect, then leaning down behind him, he whispered behind Chung's ear, "I don't have time for your fucking games. I need answers. I need them fast. And I will do whatever I have to do to get them." Preston then stood, and slowly walked out the door.

Chung didn't expect that. He thought he was going to be hit. Now he was confused by the passiveness of his interrogators. He found a thread of defiance within himself and grasped it tightly, muttering out loud, "No wonder these cowards are losing their power! They are weak."

Just then the door opened, and he realized his ordeal was far from over when two technicians wearing white lab coats walked in. One of them pushed a wheeled cart with a white sheet draped over it.

They positioned the cart behind him. One technician then grabbed Chung from behind, putting his neck in an arm hold and pressing hard on his carotid artery. In moments he passed out.

It's a very quick method of immobilizing someone—and also relatively short-lived. Both served the interrogators' purpose just fine.

Chung woke a few minutes later with a pounding headache. He recognized he was still in the same room, but now he was naked and shackled to a wire-framed chair that was secured to the floor with industrial clamps. What he didn't yet know was that the clamps would also serve as a ground. He began to understand this as he saw the technicians clip wires to the chair.

To give him a taste of the situation, and also to test the system, a pulse charge was issued from the twelve volts DC battery, but only two amps were run through the system. Chung jumped from the bite of the juice. It was quick and the low amperage produced a minimal shock, but it was noticeable all the same.

Again, the door opened and in walked Preston. He grimaced at Chung and gently took the seat across from him.

"Let's try this again, shall we? What is your name?"

With defiance and now disdain on his face, Chung repeated, "My name is Robert Lee!"

Preston nodded to the tech, who triggered a one-second burst of twelve volts and five amps. Not horrible, and far from deadly, but a good jolt of juice. Chung's jaw clinched and his muscles tightened but he recovered the defiant look all too quickly, and Preston nodded for another jolt before even asking a question. He kept that pattern going. Each time the techs increased the amperage one amp.

After the eighth shock, the look of defiance was replaced by one of futility. Acquiescence was yet to come, but it wouldn't be long.

"What is your name?" Preston asked in the same level tone.

"Jong-Kip Chung," the defiance now replaced with anger.

"Who are you working for?"

"I already told you, you dumb ass. I work for Daewoo Motor, where I drive truck!"

Preston put out his lower lip in a look of considered disappointment, and gave the tech a nod.

The jolt was now at fourteen amps, but still just one second long. Now the length would begin to increase. The goal was to get the information they wanted and not kill their only source of that information or contaminate its veracity. The heart muscle gets tricky with DC amperage, but since the electrode contacts are limited to the skin surface and kept away from the chest area, the risks can be mitigated.

Another nod, and another, now up to four seconds, and the agony can actually be smelled—or perhaps it's just the shit piled on the floor from that last one.

Preston calmly and flatly asked again, "Who do you work for?"

The anger was gone. It was replaced with self-pity and fear. Through tears of desperation, Chung said in a low voice, "They'll kill me."

"Then it seems to me, we are your best bet, because you should know that to them you are already dead. If you go back, you will not live. Your only chance is with us, and at this point I'd give that a twenty percent chance at best." For emphasis, he nodded to the tech and a four-second shock was delivered.

When it stopped, Chung slumped in the chair with his chin on his chest. For a moment, Preston thought he'd gone too far; but he knew and trusted in the abilities of the technicians. They were charged with the responsibility of delivering the appropriate level, intensity, and time of shock whenever they got a nod. Appropriate is defined as being nonlethal.

Preston slapped him on the cheek repeatedly. As Chung began to show he was back with them again, Preston said with the calm voice that by now seemed almost psychotic, "Who do you work for?"

"You know who I work for! I work for Father Kim Jong-un," Chung's response was a sad indicator that he was a brainwashed victim of North Korea's communist system, where every person is taught they are the "children" of the country's political leader. A system, much like Iran's, intended to place the leader in the exalted position of being literally a god to the people.

Preston was very pleased now. It was clear this man was not well trained. Such a devotee with the proper training would never break. He'd die before giving any information to the "evil Zionists" of the West—and Preston therefore would have to kill the man in order to validate his willingness to die.

"What was your mission?"

"Fuck you, you insect. That's what you and your kind are—locusts trying to occupy the planet and devour its resources."

Preston ignored the insult. He didn't give a shit what this brainwashed victim of an isolationist, communist regime thought of him. In truth, he knew the man wasn't capable of independent thought. The rhetoric he spewed was no more meaningful than those of a parrot that repeats learned words and phrases and recites them by rote without knowing the meaning of any of it.

Another nod to the tech and Chung found himself covered in sweat; but it wasn't enough. It was time to up the ante.

Torture is a crime and is governed by hundreds of agreements between countries in the time of war. Yet there exist no such agreements with North Korea, nor is there currently an official war with North Korea. The American people and for the most part its courts are content not knowing what goes on in these closed rooms.

The progression of torture usually depends on the personality traits of the person being tortured. Typically, there is time to formulate a personality profile so the information can be used to administer the most effective methods. Does this person respond best to humiliation, bodily harm, threats to his family? What specifically is the most effective motivator?

In the absence of such information, pain is usually the universal motivator to get someone to speak; but it's an art. You cross a certain threshold and information spills out, but it's just as likely fabrication as truth.

SWAT teams and other law enforcement agencies know that when faced with a suspect they need to have surrender, if they aim guns at the suspect's head and threaten to kill him, he will remain defiant. He will fail to surrender. If the sights are lowered to his groin, however, the suspect almost always surrenders—and quickly.

When the techs set a tray of instruments on the table, the purpose of some were obvious, while others were less so. Chung began to feel a lump in his throat. When techs began to touch his genitals, that lump rocketed to his stomach and his penis began to retract in fear. At once, a long metal rod on the tray had meaning, and it was not a pleasant thought at all.

While the technicians added hardware, Preston left, muttering, "They break. They always break. Question is, can we count on what they have to say?" On his way out, he wondered how these "techs" could do what they had to do. Looking at them now, he got an even darker feeling when he saw they actually enjoyed it.

Twenty minutes later he returned. A table had been added, set in front of Chung, so thankfully Preston couldn't see what was below the man's waist. There was a new look in his face now, one that clearly said, "I'll do whatever you want—please don't let them hurt me anymore!"

It's a type of Stockholm syndrome: one interrogator is considered a "friend" since he is the one communicating. Consequently, he's the only human being with whom the captor feels he has a connection, even though this is also the person responsible for his plight.

Gently, in the same even tone, Preston asked, "What is your mission?"

Looking down at his crotch and then up to Preston's eyes, and then over to the table, Chung responded.

JUNE 27, 20:35 KDT

USAF Camp Kim, South Korea

"**M**y mission was to drive the truck full of cars to the port. Back and forth. That's what I did. Then one day I get a message to take one load of cars the next day to a warehouse located between the factory and the port. That's it. I swear that's all I know."

Preston paused for a just a moment, considering, then gave the techs a nod. Chung saw the gears turning in Preston's head and the upward glance to the techs and he begged, "No, God no! Please don't!"

Preston broke his flat-tone delivery with a shouting tirade. "Don't you use God to beg for mercy! Or have you forgotten you forsake God? You think that crackpot despot is your god? What mercy do you think HE would show you at this moment? Your only god right now is me! I will decide if you live or die, and on what terms you live or die! Do you understand? From this point on, you have no way back. Your life, as you know it, is over. There's a new life that's possible for you, but it's tenuous at best, and dependent on your cooperation. So you better start talking and tell me everything if you even want a clue as to what your new life might look like!"

Chung looked down in shame. He glanced to his left, wondering if he could see the techs, wondering if he could somehow signal to them to end it, to put him out of his misery.

His eyes pulled back up to Preston's, and Preston saw hope. Praise God, there it was. He'd won. He'd broken him. Chung now saw Preston as his savior, his gateway to living.

"I drove the truck to the warehouse and was signaled inside. As I pulled the rig into the warehouse, I saw a whole team of people around tools, and what looked like gas tanks. There were eight of them. As soon as the doors closed, I was instructed to get out of the truck and help unload the cars. With so many people, this only took a few minutes. Then I saw them jack up the cars. They had four lifts and worked on four cars at a time."

"They replaced the gas tanks? Why did they do that?" Preston asked the questions as though Chung was a friend who would readily answer. The reply came straight away.

"I don't know why."

"How long did it take to replace the tanks?"

"No more than twenty minutes. It was like they'd done it thousands of times."

"Humph, they probably had," grunted Preston. "Then what?"

"We loaded the cars back up, and I was told to resume the delivery, but to pull over down the road and let the air out of a tire and call the dispatch for service."

"To provide an excuse for your arrival at the port so late?" asked Preston.

"Yeah, I guess."

"But what about the time up to that point? You were already way off schedule?"

"No, not really. The traffic around Busan is horrible. Our drive time can vary by as much as two hours. This whole process was around one hour," Chung explained.

Something about Chung's cooperation was beginning to strike Preston as odd. Yeah sure, guys open up when a ten-inch metal rod with wires attached is run up their penis, but the language and rhythm of speech had changed. He'd begun to use more casual English, as though he were very familiar with it.

He began to think Chung might be higher level after all. This could be good or bad. The potential good was that he might get more information about the enemy's mission. The potential bad was that he might be skilled enough to provide disinformation under torture too.

He decided it was time to use the hardware that had been installed in Chung's most private and—to the majority of men—most valuable possession. The technology was pretty simple. It was intended to leave internal damage only. Nothing would be visible outwardly, but the damage to the victim's reproductive and urinary systems could be extensive, making orgasm impossible, and causing incontinence, forcing the man to wear a diaper or a catheter the rest of his life. The metal rod was inserted down his urethra through his prostate, and right up to the bladder sphincter. It had the ability to use both infrared as well as thermal heat to torture and damage all those sensitive bits.

Similar rods, more like thin-gauge needles, were inserted into each of Chung's testicles. They too were designed to damage from the inside out, radiating heat from the needle core, how far, depending on how long it was active. The intensity wasn't adjustable; it was either on or off. It's all about how long the heat is applied.

Preston painstakingly explained the devices to Chung, informing him of their capabilities, and that they would destroy him. It is at this point a spy will decide how far he is willing to go to serve his country. While the pain of this procedure is not insignificant, it is still nothing on the order of more traditional tortures. No, the power of this process is to use the victim's primal fears and instinctual needs against him. This is psychological torture at its core.

Preston knew his man would either begin talking fast with just the slightest touch of the switch or clam up, in favor of sacrificing himself to the state. Something about him, though, led Preston to believe this would not result in the unmanning of Chung. His actions on the plane proved he wanted to live, and most desirably, as a full man.

Preston dialed a two on the digital timer, indicating a two-second "burn" of the metal cores embedded in Chung's genitals. His finger hovered over the button . . .

JUNE 28, 01:08 KDT

USAF Camp Kim, South Korea

Preston knew he'd have to apply the two-second burn. He knew Chung would not believe the machine's function until he felt it for himself.

Preston depressed the button and the machine whined as though it were a generator starting up. Once the infrared system was charged, the timer began automatically, with an electrical clunk. Chung thought it sounded like the heavy-duty switch that signaled the sauna heater had kicked on back at the training institute's gym.

Instantly, Chung felt the charge—like he was taking the most painful piss of his life, and that his nuts were about to explode from a sudden buildup of steam inside the tender glands.

He was convinced. Two seconds were an eternity, and he knew this machine would do exactly what Preston told him it would do.

His country would never forgive him. From this moment, he knew he was dead as far as his leaders were concerned. He looked at Preston and without either saying a word, the two men knew they had an accord. Chung accepted that his fate was now in the hands of his former enemy.

Though Chung was now a full-fledged informer, Preston knew he had to ask the right questions in the right way to get the answers he needed.

"OK. Let's start with how many cars were shipped with these devices in them."

"There were eight," answered Chung.

"Was the number eight chosen for any reason?"

"Numerology would be as good a reason as any," Chung offered, worried his theoretical answer would earn him more destruction.

"Were they all shipped to the same place?"

"No."

Preston reached forward and dialed a three on the machine. He wanted to get Chung to stop with his evasive and minimal answers. "This is not a court. You are not testifying. You are encouraged—no, make that *expected*—to answer with more than a yes or no!"

Chung nodded, grimacing at the machine ready and set for three seconds.

Preston pressed. "How many were shipped to each port—and which ports were they shipped to?"

"Three went to Benicia, three went to Newark, and two went to Houston."

"The three sent to Benicia ... what was their final target?"

"I don't know the final plan—I swear literally on my nuts! I overheard one was going to lay Las Vegas to ruins. They said it would be a modern-day Pompeii."

Preston wanted to confirm. "That's what you heard?"

"Yes, that is what they said, but no mention of other places, other than the ports themselves."

"Do you think the ports themselves were targets?"

"I don't think so. Only Newark and San Francisco would represent serious damage, so maybe one was intended to stay there. I honestly don't know that part of the plan," said Chung, looking downward with anxiety.

"Do you know how the vehicles are transported to their destination from the ports?"

"I know it's usually by truck or train or even in some cases a combination of both."

"How is the destination of a car determined?" asked Preston.

"I don't know all the details, but General Motors decides what dealers get what cars," explained a more-informed-than-expected Chung.

"And someone in your operation is controlling that, or has it just been left to chance?" Preston inquired.

"Not chance, no. I know there were specific targets," Chung offered cautiously.

"So, you have someone in General Motors sending specific cars to specific places?"

Chung was fearfully staring at the three-second timer. "I don't know the details, but that would be the most possible."

"You don't know to what places?" probed Preston.

Chung, staring at the digital number three on the timer, swallowed then lifted his head to look Preston right in the eyes to answer, hoping in doing so this man would see he was telling the truth. "No, other than Las Vegas, I don't know." He slumped back, resigned to getting his genitals fried.

Preston saw the fear, noticed Chung's desperate attempt to indicate his desire to be seen as truthful, and decided he was getting more now with the threat of long-term damage alone.

"Do all of the cars have the same device installed?" asked Preston.

"I think that's the case. I don't know for certain, though," Chung said thoughtfully.

"Do you know the capability of the weapon?"

"Not the technical specifications, but the things I'd heard about Las Vegas was that it would destroy or damage most of the garish hotels that city is known for," Chung said, just a little too boastfully.

Preston's eyes widened. Since he had yet to be told what the team in Benicia had discovered, he hadn't even considered the possibility that what he was questioning Chung about was a nuclear device.

Preston considered this for a moment and began to wonder if he'd been too gentle with Chung. No, no, he knew he had to keep his anger in check and get the information he could. He was told this was their one and only lead.

While trying to hide the shock in his voice, he asked Chung, "These bombs are nuclear?"

Now it was Chung's turn to look surprised. He had no idea the American didn't already know what was in the gas tanks of the Korean Chevys. He couldn't help himself. He felt the corners of his mouth move up into a grin. He didn't consciously want to smile. In fact, the very moment he felt it happening, he regretted it.

Preston saw the grin and lost control. It was just more than he could push down inside himself. This asshole was taking pride in the prospect of eight nuclear devices being detonated in populated areas, killing millions and making millions more suffer a variety of illnesses for the rest of their lives? He punched the button.

Almost immediately he regretted it. As Chung writhed in the chair and sweat broke on his face, shoulders and chest, he knew he'd have to make the next threat even more terrifying to counter the hatred he just engendered.

The moment Chung mentally revived, Preston dialed a seven into the machine. He wanted Chung to know that regardless of his hatred he'd be well advised to keep cooperating.

"So, again, to confirm, these are nuclear devices we're talking about?" Preston asked, his tone demanding.

Chung didn't smile. "Yes. I thought you already knew that."

JUNE 28, 06:21 KDT

USAF Camp Kim, South Korea

The light in the room flickered, signaling Preston to come out; a subtle signal. In such a crude environment, a power interruption would hardly be noticed by a detainee. This place in fact was intentionally built to appear crude.

"I am going to give you a short break. When I come back, I expect to find out how you expect me to believe your country has the capability to build eight nuclear bombs and plant them in eight cars bound for the United States!"

The door's electronic lock clicked open and Preston left the room. He was met by Director Kim. Preston looked at him as though he wondered how the hell he'd gotten in, then he remembered that Kim was very well respected by the director of this facility, an air force brigadier general by the name of Steve Kessler, who was standing right next to Kim.

Kessler was a gritty man with leathery skin who didn't feel it necessary to use a lot of words. In a gravelly voice that sounded as though he'd either smoked a million cigarettes or spent the day on horseback riding the desert with no water, Kessler grumbled, "We've got more info from the states. I'd call it intelligence, but I am always suspect of that term."

Preston cracked a grin and quickly asked, "Is Director Kim cleared?"

"Yeah, he's clear. And I'll tell you what, you're right to ask. I've been told the usual channels are closed on this," Kessler said.

"So, what's the latest from the states? The device is a nuke?" asked Preston.

Kessler was both impressed and surprised, but he was not amused. "When did you find out?"

"About twenty minutes ago. I was just getting a bit more detail. How tight is this circle? Who's out and who's in?"

"I don't know who's out, but I do know we can speak with Craig Stout, Director Richards, Dr. Kim, and the president. And that's damn near about it!" explained Kessler.

"Bonner seems to be an obvious omission," Preston noted.

Kessler offered a shrug in response.

Preston shifted his feet, concerned. "Well," he grunted, "then I'll give credibility to my informant. We can skip the usual psych and analysis bullshit, I don't think we have fucking time for it."

Preston filled in Kessler and Kim on what he'd found so far. It was a quick conversation, with him talking and the others listening with increasing alarm.

The usually quiet Kessler began to turn red, anger seething from his pores. "You mean to tell me these little fuckers have put eight nukes in the U.S. and we don't know where they are or when they will detonate?" As he spoke, he realized Kim was right there. "Fuck," he said, embarrassed. "I'm sorry. You know I don't disrespect any race."

Kim, always honest, regardless of how ugly or hurtful the truth, spoke low. "Even words said in anger have an element of truth, but I accept your apology."

It was clear to everyone these words soaked in. Preston broke the awkward moment. "That's where we are now, yes sir!" He pointed to the interrogation room. "He's sweating it out now, but I doubt he's got much more for us. I think we've gotta get someone in Detroit. The trail seems headed toward General Motors HQ."

Kessler thoughtfully looked at the ceiling and said quietly to Preston, "You've got a report to make to Richards. Use my office, and make sure you secure the line."

JUNE 27, 17:38 EDT

FBI Headquarters, Washington, D.C.

Richards hung up after getting Preston's report. This was the doomsday scenario everyone trained for in both U.S. intelligence services and all the military branches—the very scenario scoffed at and scorned by citizen watchdog groups and even Congress as paranoid fabrications. Even he had certain doubts. Was this in fact one of those moments? More to the point, were they truly prepared?

Terrifying thoughts for a man who right now held the fragile hope of mitigating such a threat. "This is useless. Get back to it, old man," he told himself, picking up the phone to call Craig Stout.

It's not the usual chain of command for the director to call a subordinate about making assignments in an investigation, but Richards was putting all his chips on the table. His opinion: there was one chance for success, and that was for Stout to continue to head the investigation. Craig knew people at his level he could trust, giving him a huge advantage over Richards himself; and too it's what the president wanted.

JUNE 28, 07:44 KDT

USAF Camp Kim, South Korea

As he entered the interrogation room, Preston saw Chung still staring at his crotch, strapped into the wire chair—wondering, no doubt, if his genitals were already ruined.

Preston thought that he'd better reassure the man they probably were not—but that could change with one touch of the button.

He approached Chung and sat at the table across from him.

"You're wondering if the damage is already done, if there's any point in cooperating any further. Let me assure you, many men have not only survived what you've been through but have survived fully functional. That does, however, *change* with each treatment. Not only will the time increase, but the damage is also exponential with each push of the button. Do you understand?"

Chung nodded, almost eagerly, with a sense of glee in a way.

And Preston knew he'd not have to use the machine again.

"You were about to tell me how such a piss-poor country like North Korea was able to pull this off. It had to have cost millions, if not billions."

"I am not in the circle of . . ." Chung paused, searching for the right expression or word, ". . . *knowing*, is that right?"—instantly seeking confirmation that his English was understood, lest that button get pressed.

Preston nodded. "Yeah, that's it, go ahead. I understand."

"I only heard, you know, talk, bullshit maybe, that it was help from another country, with both the enriched plutonium and also money. I think our part was limited to accessing and shipping the packages into the U.S.," Chung quickly explained.

"OK, makes sense, but what country?"

"I don't know—I mean, I never was told what country."

"Don't make me push that button. You have a better idea than I do right now what country, and you'd better be singing like a bird at this point," threatened Preston.

Chung's fear was evident again, but he also felt like he had reached his end, the point where he couldn't cope with this anymore, and now wondered if he would be killed anyway. He'd been told by his trainers that if he was captured, the Americans would kill him. Now, though, there was doubt, and he began to think he might not be killed after all.

"We all just assumed it was Iran," said Chung.

"Were there any signs of that? Something you saw that helped confirm it?"

"I didn't have any interaction with the people who assembled the bombs, but when I was helping install them in the cars, there was some foreign writing on some of the parts," said Chung.

"Arabic?"

"I don't know, but it wasn't Korean or Chinese or English. There were dots and dashes, over and around characters with squiggly, curved lines."

That was good enough for Preston.

"These cars, you said you don't know where they were going to end up, exactly, but you thought someone at GM was part of the plan to get them to the right places. What makes you say that?"

"From my time at Daewoo I learned that cars are shipped either to the port or to dealers in Korea, based on what the computer printed out on the sticker that was on the window of the car. Someone has to tell the computer what to print." His shrug indicated to Preston that "someone" was unknown to Chung.

"OK."

Preston was satisfied. Chung could give him nothing more.

"You know you will never go home again. To live, there will be a long period of time in which you'll need to convince us you have turned willingly, and with complete integrity, and that you will never betray or sabotage the United States."

Chung nodded and looked down again, hoping Preston would instruct the techs to disconnect him.

JUNE 27, 15:45 PDT

Benicia, California

Benicia, California, had not experienced the increase in development that had been so prevalent in the bulk of the Bay Area. Its relative isolation made for an impractical commute to San Francisco or Oakland. As a receiving port for automobiles, it would appear at first glance to be less than strategic, which is somewhat true for truck traffic taking processed cars into San Francisco. This processing center was also responsible, however, for distribution of Korean-built Chevrolet cars to dealers throughout most of the Western United States. The railhead attached to the far end of the facility and the port's relative isolation made this location perfect for the port's original mission: to handle the shipping of munitions from the West Coast to the Pacific front during World War II.

The irony wasn't missed by Craig, as he looked out at the brown waters rich with silt from the Sacramento River that empties here on its final journey to the Pacific Ocean. He didn't think for a moment the parties responsible for the bomb even knew.

As he pressed End to finish the call with Director Richards, Craig gazed over these waters in deep reflection, an activity he ordinarily considered a waste of time. Now, though, confronted with the angel of death, he paused to consider life.

He'd just learned that this bomb was likely part of a much larger operation, perhaps even a nation-wide conspiracy. That alone caused him to wonder if the director was in on it too—and if so, was there no one he could trust? *Shake it off!* he told himself. *You can't afford to get paranoid.*

There were no leads, nothing to follow on his end. He had to find out more, and fast. The one person he could trust was Scott; and being the president's son—who also happened to be in charge of the NSA's Economic Terrorism Unit—he had the necessary clearance.

Craig called Scott at the office but got his voicemail. He left a message requesting a call back ASAP. Then he paged him on the emergency system, knowing he'd get that in minutes. On a whim, he thought he'd try the home number and was surprised when Scott picked up.

"Hey, what's up? And where are you?"

Then Craig realized it was almost 19:00 in D.C., and began to do some damage control of his own. "Damn, babe, I'm sorry. I'm near San Francisco. There's a situation here."

Scott broke in. "Yeah, I know. There's always a situation. I knew what I signed up for with you, but I thought I'd see you at least once in a while."

Craig knew this wasn't going to be fixed now, so he appealed to the desire to be needed, which was very true: he needed Scott's expertise now. "I know. I know. My communication with you sucks, I'm sorry, you deserve better from me; but can we please talk about that later? I need your help. I think this might be the crisis we've trained for, the one we fear but hope will never happen. You know the one?"

Scott switched gears. It was amazing how he could do that—and one big part of why they worked. "Shit. What's going on?"

"That line isn't secure. I need you to call me back on the scrambled SAT phone in the closet. Here's the number: nine nine nine-five five five-one one one one. Code: nine eight eight four five nine three seven. That code will only work from that SAT phone."

"I'll call in five minutes, and sorry about earlier. You sound genuinely scared," said Scott.

"Forget it, don't apologize when I'm the one who's been an ass." Craig ended the call. He didn't mean to be short, but it bothered him that Scott could read him that way. He was trained not to signal emotion. He feared when Scott could do it, he might be losing his edge.

Scott's return call at first added to that fear, starting with, "You know I can always tell when you're scared," but Craig relaxed as soon as he heard "what I hope is someday that will be OK with you." At that point Craig knew he was not alone. He had an ally. Scott knowing him so well did make him feel safe, not easy to admit for a man whose self-imposed obligation was to make others feel safe.

He proceeded to run through the day, all the events, the flight interception in Korea, the knowledge gained from the spy on that plane; and the fear it was all orchestrated with either the tacit knowledge of Bonner or even worse, masterminded by him. Craig went even further, telling Scott that the director didn't disavow the idea that the president himself could be involved.

Scott didn't take any of this personally; he knew how it would look from the perspective of those paid to do the looking. Yet he was confident in his belief that his dad had no knowledge of this. He hadn't the slightest doubt.

Scott summarized what he'd heard to confirm he'd heard correctly. It seemed unreal. "So, what we know is that a spy posed as a truck driver at this car factory in South Korea for years. And that four weeks ago he was instructed through his control to detour delivery of a truckload of specific cars to a warehouse located a mile short of the port. He pulled the truck and trailer inside, where he saw a few dozen men, and four car lifts, and what appeared to be an automotive shop rack filled with spare gas tanks."

"So far that's it, yeah . . ."

"And we know he drove that load of cars to the port, showing up a few minutes later than expected, and the company's GPS had recorded that the truck had stopped for precisely fifty-one minutes on its way to the port. And then he called for service just short of the port, due to a flat tire. OK, so the cars go on to the port for shipping. We know the gas tanks were changed out and assume the explosive devices were already installed in the replacement gas tanks," said Scott.

"Yeah, that's right so far," Craig replied, rolling his eyes at calling a nuke an "explosive device." Analysts, he thought, can be so dispassionate as to sound absurd at times.

"You are in possession of one car, have defused the bomb, and are in the process of finding out where the nuclear material was sourced from, if it's in our databases. So ... what do you need me for?" asked Scott.

"What do you think?" asked Craig. "You don't do a job like this on a budget. Everyone looking at this device says it's top-notch. There was nothing crude or rudimentary about it. This was clearly the work of someone with serious resources."

"Ah, so you need to figure out who bankrolled a multimillion-dollar plot, and how they paid the many experts that would have been involved?"

"Yeah, but I have a feeling this was limited to very few experts. This was so clandestine, it never came up on anyone's radar until a car showed up in one of our ports capable of annihilating a city. This had to be tightly controlled. You can only do that by limiting the number of people involved," said Craig.

"Unless you simply kill them when you are done with them," Scott grumbled, "something right out of the KGB playbook."

"That would be another logical option. Besides the money, we better look into missing scientists in the fields of metallurgy, electronics, and nuclear technology. There's still a lot we don't even know about this device. The detonator, for example, seems as though it was designed to be radio controlled, perhaps with a cellular signal; or some other signal would most likely arm it, making it go live."

"OK, I'll get the ears on. You thinking we need to keep a lid on this still?"

Craig pursed his lips, knowing his boss was weighing the risk of the public getting wind of this against the risk of speeding the investigation. "Our first priority is to confirm if we are dealing with multiple devices. We're reasonably confident our information on that is good, but I want to know for sure, and if there are more, where they are. Once we know this threat is contained, we can get the lid back on it. There won't be a public need to know."

Ever the pragmatist, Scott interjected, "And if it's not the only device? How the hell do we get a lid back on it then?"

"I wouldn't worry too much about that," said Craig. "If there are more, public hysteria will be the least of our problems. We'll be fucked."

"I'll put out a blanket dispatch then to all friendly investigative operations worldwide, including Interpol. I'll keep it vague and nonspecific, saying we're trying to root out a massive money laundering scheme. Also, I'm going to get clearance from the top for you to stay lead on this," said Scott.

"I understand, but what the hell am I supposed to do if someone up the ladder relieves me?"

"Once I have the authority I intend to get, there's just one person who can relieve you and that would be my dad. And be careful. If this has the conspiracy aspect you suspect, someone might be interested in doing whatever they can to impede you and your investigation."

"You worry too much," said Craig.

"Well *someone* has to seem like they are worried," Scott shot back, "and you usually give me plenty to worry about."

JUNE 27, 17:08 PDT

Benicia, California

That last statement was still resounding in Craig's ears. While it occurred to him that he'd become a target if he got too close to the source of the conspiracy, the reality that someone might come gunning for him wasn't a comfortable thought. Shaking his head clear, he decided to focus on the things he could control for now.

As far as trusting that the president wasn't involved, Craig just couldn't give anyone a free pass in the investigation, even someone he considered to be a father. Trust wasn't something Craig believed in. He neither expected others to trust him nor trusted anyone else, even people he worked for; just because you were higher up the food chain didn't mean you'd earned this officer's trust.

As for his feelings, those had changed since being with Scott. He realized that he *wanted* to believe the president wasn't involved. That was new. Now he had to hope it didn't turn out to be a weakness.

Something about the Secretary of Homeland Security always gave Craig the willies—even from when he was a college student. Bonner had come onto the political scene pretty much out of nowhere; as a result of the disastrous response to Hurricane Katrina in New Orleans by the previous administration, he had been appointed to replace one of the many incompetent cronies qualified for his position solely on the merits of being a good ol' boy.

Coming in, Bonner gave off an arrogant air, of being Teflon coated; you could read it in his eyes: *If they only knew what I am capable of.* To Craig, it seemed, here was a guy more than comfortable with deception, well-rehearsed in its arts, who appeared to be operating in a state of avoidance with the tacit approval of those who had hired him. His actions, as well as those of the new DHS, were anything but transparent.

After 9/11, people demanded action and looked to the government for leadership. The administration's response early on had been to create the Department of Homeland Security, bringing different agencies together under one umbrella, agencies that historically didn't get along and rarely shared information. Clearly, it was felt that culture had to change, lest the country suffer further catastrophic attacks. Deterrence now depended on a level of interagency and interdepartmental cooperation previously unknown and never before tried. Law enforcement was to enter a new phase.

Compared to Europeans, Americans are not familiar with the pain of war, the real pain. Most only know that fear from images on TV and stories in books. Even Pearl Harbor, as devastating as it was, happened far away, preventing most Americans from seeing it firsthand. It wasn't until September 2001 that Americans were witnesses on an epic scale to how an attack can feel—and that was only one day.

What happened after that is well known. A long time has passed since the American Revolution, what was fought for and won, and what patriots did to protect it. Meanings change, especially the meaning of words. A *patriot*, for instance, at one time meant a fighter who fought against tyranny, against an unjust system of government. This often meant fighting to the death, for liberty and what was then known as the common good. More than one war was fought toward that end.

After September 11, that meaning changed, and the word was deployed toward a different end, one that redefined freedom and what that might entail. Overnight there appeared the Patriot Act, alongside the newly empowered Department of Homeland Security. A calculation was made in the name of the American people by which "a certain amount" of liberty was traded for the appearance and allure of safety. The irony that Patriots gave their lives for our liberty, was not lost for critics of the Act.

Michael Bonner, in any case, was onboard.

JUNE 27, 18:41 PDT

Benicia, California

"I know I am in California! Do you forget I'm the one who about killed myself getting here?!" Craig yelled into the SAT phone, something not ordinarily said to the boss, especially not the director of the CIA—but nothing was ordinary about this case. "I am going to Detroit. There is nothing more for me to do here."

"You have to trust that someone else can get the answers," explained Director Richards. "You can't do everything yourself. There are other capable people you can count on!"

"Don't turn this into that. I am no egomaniac, you know that. I let Preston conduct the interrogation of the North Korean. I know my limits and know what's best in this investigation, too. Right now, I am the closest person to Detroit I trust with this!"

"All right, then get your ass there. What do you want done ahead of your arrival?"

Craig thought a moment. "Get a good guy, but someone junior. I don't want people with connections in the agency, we need to keep a lid on this. A by-the-book rookie. Get him into General Motors headquarters, have him meet with the CEO, and get anyone and everyone responsible for distribution of vehicles from the port to dealers in a closed and locked room. No bathroom breaks that aren't supervised. I want them on suicide watch, total isolation, until I get there. I'll take this SAT phone with me. Have the agent you assign call me for more specific instructions while he is en route to GM. Will you take care of the CEO?"

"I'll call him right now. I hope he's in Detroit," said Richards.

"If he is anywhere near Detroit, get him there immediately. We'll need his authority to keep this as quiet as possible."

"He's not going to be pleased with this."

"Before this is over, he won't be alone," groused Craig. "Do me a favor and pull some strings at Travis Air Force base. Get me the fastest plane they have to Detroit. I'll be there in twenty minutes."

JUNE 27, 19:17 PDT

Benicia, California

This was Craig Stout's second no-frills flight in fewer than forty-four hours. Sleep was not even in the equation, but maybe he could nod off for a few minutes. The noise-canceling headphones and microphones on the Air Force jets are the best such technology in the world. Bose charges close to $300 for the consumer version frequent fliers use on commercial flights. The Air Force version cost nearly twenty times that, and it was worth every penny.

By the time Stout climbed into the rear first officer's seat of the long-range F-18, it'd been eighteen minutes since he'd spoken with Richards. It took him two minutes to put on the insulated flight suit, a godsend at the altitudes they were going to be flying, to take advantage of the thinner air for maximum speed.

He no sooner got the helmet on when the SAT phone began to ring. The canopy was lowered and they would be airborne in minutes, reaching g-forces that would make speaking impossible until they leveled off.

"Stout here. You are on a secure line."

"It's Richards. Your agent is Zach Thompson. He's with the FBI in Detroit. They have more judicial power within our borders. Don't worry. I know him. He'll report to you exclusively. It's bad enough we've got you and a half-dozen other CIA officers now doing what amounts to illegal ops inside the country."

"Yeah, yeah, OK, fine," Craig couldn't be bothered with politics. "Have him call me in twelve minutes. We're about to take off."

"Fine. I've not been able to reach the CEO of GM yet. He's harder to get on the phone than the president. I'll give Thompson his contact info."

"Our flight plan is one hour forty-two minutes."

"Yeah," Richards admitted, "I doubt we could've gotten someone else there much sooner, but you need rest soon, too."

"I'll rest when I'm dead, and if we don't get this in hand that may be very soon for us all."

Richards ended the call. He wasn't worried. He knew Stout was as alert after forty-eight hours of nonstop ops as any other man after a good night's sleep. He didn't put the phone in the cradle, though; rather, he asked the operator for a secure line and waited for a dial tone. Once he had it, he redialed the office of GM's CEO, Robert Smith.

"Hello, you've reached Mr. Smith's office. He's not available. Leave a message and your call will be returned as soon as possible," stated the professional yet tough recorded voice of Sarah Cohen, Smith's executive assistant. At this time of night, there would be no point in leaving a message. Richards next called the NSA and asked for Smith's cell phone number, retrieved in less than a minute.

After several rings he heard, "Robert Smith. What is it, Sarah?" expecting his loyal assistant.

"Mr. Smith, this is Director Steven Richards of the CIA."

There followed silence, then, "Sorry for the pause. What can I do for you?"

"First, I need to impress upon you that this is a matter of national security. You are not to tell anyone you've spoken with me. You are not to tell anyone the real reason for the actions I am about to ask you to take. I hope you are a convincing liar, Mr. Smith."

"I am the CEO of a major corporation, Mr. Richards, so probably as skilled in that regard as a senator."

"That qualifies." Richards was glad someone still had some humor, but in a moment that would change, maybe forever. "Your company is involved in a national crisis the scope of which I can't fully disclose to you. But I can tell you someone in your distribution department is an enemy of the state."

The silence on the line was broken by Richards asking, "Are you there, Mr. Smith?"

"Yeah, yeah, I'm here, sorry ... I don't know what to say or even how to react right now, I'm stunned. I think I need to know more about what's happening."

"Mr. Smith, trust me when I say you don't want to know a thing about what's happening, the less you know the better off you will be."

Another short silence. "Well, I can't say that eases my mind at all!"

"It's not my objective to ease your mind, Mr. Smith. I'm sorry, but that's the brutal, unvarnished truth."

Smith exhaled a sigh. "I don't need any details. In fact, I guess this is one of those occasions when there are advantages to ignorance in terms of, what do you people call it, plausible deniability?"

This and other reminders that top CEOs are the same political animals as those with whom Richards has to deal in Washington wasn't lost on him. Here, though, the balance of power was much more in his court.

"Can we depend on the full cooperation of your company?"

"Within limits, of course," said Smith, keen to maintain control.

"No, sir. With all due respect, this situation demands the full cooperation of you, General Motors, and its entire staff. This is not a negotiation. It is to our advantage and I daresay yours as well that we come in under the radar, get what we need, involve as few people as necessary, and disrupt your organization as little as possible."

Smith realized it was time to be a patriot and be able to claim he in no way hindered the investigation, and to be helpful to the government in every way imaginable. "My assistant will greet your people on arrival and provide them with whatever access they need."

"That's not going to do it. You know as well as I do that top executives and middle managers will be reluctant to leave their desks at the demand of your assistant. I am sure they respect her but I need you there by morning."

"That's not going to be easy. I'm currently at our factory in Silao, Mexico. Even if I left right now, we have customs, and my pilot has to get a takeoff slot; then there is the twenty- to twenty-five-minute car ride to my office," Smith explained.

"Don't worry about customs. You'll be met at the airport in Detroit and escorted through. I'll see what I can do with the Mexican authorities as well. So, if you please, leave right now," directed Richards.

Smith had lingering doubts. Could this be a well-organized, elaborate hostage-taking plan? Only someone high up in the government can circumvent airport security and U.S. Customs; still, he felt some trepidation.

"I also need you to think about how you will get the entire distribution department away from their desks without them alerting one another they have been summoned. They must be isolated in one room, ideally with internal restroom facilities, so we can secure their movement entirely while we investigate. Most critically, they must be—with no notice—shut off from their computer access: no way for them to issue any *kill* command that would wipe their entry history," Richards said.

"We do have a robust security team and sophisticated I.T. department. I'll work with those teams on my flight to Detroit. It might be best to work with the I.T. department first, to see if they can cut off access to that department. I'll ask them to investigate for any hidden automatic wipe code and their ideas about how to protect the system."

Richards thanked him and added, "Good thinking. Maybe they can create a restore point before shutting off the department, just in case?"

"I'll explain that it's critical we preserve any data as it is at this moment. They'll know the best way to accomplish that," Smith said.

"That may all be well and good," said Richards, "but I don't want anyone hearing about anything until we have people there. Someone from the FBI will be there before you arrive, and that person will need to vet the personnel in I.T. We'll need access to your personnel files, to get that going ASAP."

Faced with the enormity of what he was being asked to do, Smith considered for a moment. "You'll have access to anything you want within the company," he said.

"Thank you" said Richards, "that will certainly help. A lot."

JUNE 28, 07:36 EDT

Detroit, Michigan

Smith's plan was to send an internal message to each of the five women, including the department supervisor, responsible for the allocation of vehicles to dealers. Prior to that, however, security officers would be stationed in sight of each of the women, by which time I.T. would have done what it needed to do.

Each dealer has an allocation of vehicles that is determined by the number sold in the past eighteen or so months. The number of months can vary, and allocations can be changed to reward or punish dealers; but the system as a whole is based on this practice of "turn and earn." Hot-selling cars can be moved, for example, to dealers who have done well in selling more "distress" merchandise, or to dealers who excel in any number of other performance matrixes. In other words, if a car that was supposed to go to one dealer ends up at another, there would be no red flag, nothing in the system to alert anyone.

JUNE 28, 08:42 EDT

Detroit, Michigan

C raig Stout arrived in Detroit in the middle of the night, knowing that little could be done until GM's CEO arrived back from Mexico and GM's headquarters began its daily operations. The FBI man, Zach Thompson, had met him at Selfridge Air National Guard Base forty-five minutes north of Detroit and drove him to the Renaissance Center downtown. In addition to housing GM's corporate headquarters, the RenCen also housed a full-service Marriott hotel. Craig knew his mind and body needed some down time and he took full advantage of his four hours.

Robert Smith described his plan to a refreshed Craig Stout, complete with a new set of clothes Zach had provided. The plan was fairly simple: send internal instant messages to the five employees of the allocation department then monitor their movements as they proceeded to the CEO's office. If an employee attempted to make a phone call, her phone would be disabled. If the employee stopped at the restroom on her way, she would be discreetly followed. If the person tried to leave the building, she would be intercepted by building security and escorted to the security office under the guise she was suspected of stealing company property.

As far as the heads up to security, this department was being investigated for leaking corporate information to a competitor.

General Motors, like every major corporation in the technology age, has the ability to monitor nearly every area of its offices. Rather than a fully manned security staff, whose cost is prohibitive, it's only a matter of a few switches and key punches to activate cameras in a given area and watch employees' movements in real time.

Stout, introduced as a digital data theft consultant, watched with Smith as each employee received the message.

Every recipient of this message reacted the same way, except for one.

JUNE 28, 09:12 EDT

Detroit, Michigan

All the employees who received the message did pretty much the same thing: they looked around, stood up, paced back and forth for a second and either rubbed their forehead, ears or chin or dug fingers into hair on the back of the head—all signs of stress, indicators of anxiousness. One woman merely seemed irritated she was being called out of her routine, perhaps the least suspicious reaction of all.

Then, proceeding to the elevators, they would avoid eye contact with anyone encountered along the way. Two women stopped at the restroom, one to relieve her bladder, and the other, it was reported, to throw up.

One employee did not look around and did not show signs of stress. She pressed a few keys on her keyboard—later determined to be a command to erase her hard drive—then stood up, took her purse, and pretended to head to the restroom but instead took the elevator. Down.

On seeing the doors close and pressing L for Lobby, imagine her surprise when she felt the car lift instead. At that, she pulled a handgun from her purse. Now it was Smith's turn to look surprised. To Stout, though, her outward calmness had indicated from the beginning that this woman was not what she appeared to be.

Still, Craig put on a show for the others in the room to support his current role of security consultant. "God, this woman's a nutcase!"

Four FBI agents, including Zach Thompson, were stationed in the lobby of the RenCen as part of an "antiterrorism exercise." Like it or not, Stout was now about to tell the GM security detail an entirely new lie.

"Guys, I am actually with the FBI. This woman is wanted by the IRS for tax evasion and by the FBI for money laundering. I just signaled four of FBI's finest to proceed to this floor. They were in the lobby, but if they aren't in an elevator yet, can you expedite a car? Bring them to this floor and shut down the car containing our prisoner until the team can get into position. Make it quick!"

The thought she'd commit suicide was now Stout's most pressing concern. He needed her alive. The FBI team knew it, and hopefully they'd get to her in time.

Her car arrived at the security level but didn't open. She remained with her gun pointed at the doors, indicating that for now, at least, she didn't plan on suicide.

The FBI team's elevator car arrived twelve seconds later, and they were in position within four seconds. Most people by now would think they were trapped in the elevator, that it had malfunctioned. An idea came to Stout. He turned on the speaker in the elevator. "Is there anyone in this car?" A seemingly stupid question, since everyone knew there were cameras in elevators, but it was important that she believe this car was broken. He needed her to put away the gun.

His ruse seemed to be working. She composed herself, relaxed, but didn't yet return the gun to her purse. She did, however, pick up the phone. "Is anyone there?" she asked.

"Yes," Craig's voice crackled. "We're sorry, but the elevators are malfunctioning. We weren't even sure if someone was there."

"Aren't there cameras?"

"Seems they are on the fritz also, ma'am. We're glad the phone is working. We've got a crew on the way. They'll release the doors manually. Should be just a few minutes."

"OK, fine," she said, sounding more annoyed than scared.

"You want me to stay on the line with you until they get there?"

She rolled her eyes with the irritated look of a woman who hated men thinking she need to be taken care of. "No, I'm perfectly fine!" She hung up. Since the man on the phone sounded relaxed and confident, with no hesitation in his voice, she believed him. She slid the gun back in her purse.

She stood back and looked at the doors, willing them to open.

When they did, she hardly had time to see what was in front of her before something hit her in the chest so hard it knocked the wind from her lungs. She fell back and slid down the wall, limp as a rag doll.

JUNE 28, 09:32 EDT

Detroit, Michigan

Rezeya Kundi, the supervisor of allocation at General Motors, was a Pakistani immigrant, or so everyone at the company had been led to believe.

Craig Stout had to deal with less than ideal facilities for Ms. Kundi's interrogation. The FBI field office in Detroit was not equipped for the sort of sophisticated techniques that had been so effective with Jong-Kip Chung in Asia.

Even so, Craig thought, *I doubt those techniques would work on her anyway.*

Craig had sent word to his partner in life and the NSA's chief expert on economic terrorism to meet him in Detroit ASAP.

Not that they were able to greet each other with a hug and kiss as they yearned to, but they were still very happy to see each other.

"I'm not sure I want to be a part of this process. I don't think I have the stomach for it," Scott confided to Craig.

"Well, this isn't going to be what you fear. Yeah, we do that kind of work, but women respond differently to interrogation. They have different motivators."

"How so?" questioned Scott.

"Self-preservation for women is statistically less relevant—that is, if you believe the bulk of statistics that show women are much more likely to commit suicide, or sacrifice themselves for another. Even more than that, though, pain doesn't work on women the same way it does on men. Plus, there's the devotion factor," explained Craig.

"Ah, you mean that death isn't a detriment to her, like it was to Chung in Asia?"

"That's part of it. Chung not only wanted to live, but he also didn't feel a level of devotion to the cause, at least not at the level he was willing to trade his life for that devotion."

"Why?"

"He grew up in North Korea, being indoctrinated with all of Kim Jong-il's rhetoric claiming how much better off the people in the North were, that they didn't have to deal with stress or decisions about how to live, or where to live, or even worry about a job. That their society was a sanctuary of fairness and equality. His devotion was already fractured, otherwise I don't think we would have ever broken him, he would have died with his secrets."

"Can't we do that with Rezeya?"

"When Chung was on that flight, it was obvious to agent Lim that he was not just nervous but uncertain who even to trust," said Craig.

"Oh yeah, that flight. You know there's still shit hitting the fan over that?" Scott complained wryly, indicating pride in what Craig had accomplished.

"I don't doubt it, but I also don't give a crap," Craig returned slyly.

"If the seeds were already planted with Chung," Scott wondered, "how do you get Rezeya to turn?"

"That, my friend, is why you're here," said Craig with his goofiest grin—the one he knew Scott loved.

"Me? What can I do?"

"You can dive deep into her life. I want to know everything about her. Start with what you know and work backward. I want to know when her father planted his seed in her mother, where they were, what time of day it was, if it was passionate or brutal . . . you get the drift? Oh—and I need all of that yesterday."

"I already guessed!"

"I plan to start talking with her, see if I can even begin to engage."

Craig left for the interrogation room, of the type found in any police station. Scott headed over to I.T. He was about to take it over under the authority of the president of the United States.

JUNE 28, 13:10 EDT

Detroit, Michigan

Detroit is a major gateway to the United States, with two international border crossings with Canada, one of which is accessed from Jefferson Avenue right next to the GM Renaissance Center. In addition, Detroit Wayne International Airport is a gateway to several overseas destinations.

Most people are surprised that this small city has offices for the FBI, Secret Service, DEA, CBP, ATF, DoJ and many other federal departments, but this is due to its strategic location, not size. Scott was impressed with both the caliber of talent and level of technology at his disposal.

One call to his supervisor at the NSA with the president's authority is all it took to command the agency's supercomputer, a machine that is always on and working, with a backlog of four weeks' worth of work waiting for it.

To call this Cray a mere supercomputer would be an insult to its power and capability, not to mention price. For what it cost in energy to run (and moreover to cool), the agency could buy a new one every year.

Once Scott was connected via the field office's secure net connection (precursor to the internet, but with much more restricted access), he was able to submit queries to the NSA computer. These were basically *what if* scenarios and the computer would search its databases with logic. Yes, in a manner of speaking, it could think.

Scott typed, *Who is Rezeya Kundi, Social Security Number: 325-45-9876, Michigan Driver's License Number 123409877, General Motors Employee Number 987456, known residence Southfield, Michigan, known to live in Pakistan, Married to Said Kundi, believed to have been born March 12, 1968*, and pressed Enter.

Any search engine is highly capable, and they are getting better and better every day; but Computer (so named by its Trekkie engineers) would take each separate inquiry, find the answers, then relate them all before cross-referencing with every police, commercial, government, and even hacked database in the world. Computer could comprehend that *believed to have been born* on a certain date was different from the phrase *DOB*, and could question the results of that query as though it were a question, and look for other information that might be more accurate.

It is not the exclusive domain of criminals to use malware planted on computers that effectively turn the computer into a "bot" or a slave to another computer when connected to the internet. Criminals use them to gather personal banking and credit card information for the purposes of fraud, yet some of these "viruses" are written for the NSA. They plant themselves on mainframes and personal computers around the world and if they find data deemed of relevance, they send it to Computer.

Scott got up, knowing the computer would be chewing on the query for a while. "I need a coffee," he said to the empty room, locking the keyboard with his password.

JUNE 28, 13:25 EDT

Detroit, Michigan

"Mrs. Kundi? Is it all right if I call you Mrs. Kundi?" Craig inquired politely. She ignored him, not even giving an indication that she'd heard him.

"Mrs. Kundi, we are going to be spending all of our time together for as long as it takes. I hope you don't think for a moment that reality is any more palatable to me than it is for you."

She casually took a deep breath, let it out slowly, and remained silent. Her unambiguous body language said, *You can keep me here forever. I'll never say a word.*

Craig looked exhausted, and that didn't help his situation one bit. Rezeya got the impression she could easily outlast him.

"When did you start to work at GM?" Craig asked.

No answer.

"How long have you been in the United States?"

Nothing.

"How many friends have you made here?"

Silence.

"Did you make any friends? Or was everyone to you just a meaningless actor in your play?"

A sideways glance and an audible sigh.

"I am sure many of the people you went to school with or worked with, maybe even your neighbors, considered you a friend."

No response.

"But to you they were no more than pawns, bit pieces you could use and later discard. Merely expendable pieces in your game of strategy and revenge?"

A bodily movement, a repositioning in the chair and shifting of the arms, ending with her folding them even more tightly across her chest. That last bit struck a nerve. Something was making her uncomfortable. Was it the reference to the pawns or mention of revenge? Only one way to find out.

"Is that true? The people who took you into their hearts, who believed you were a good person, a friend, were just stepping-stones for you, useful to you just for your cover?"

"You are all the same, with your arrogant Western Judeo–Christian thought. You think you are the only ones who value human life, who treasure the beauty of life and friendship and love," she said defiantly.

"Maybe it seems that way because of your eagerness to take others' lives even if it means sacrificing a few of your own," Craig said. "Maybe Western cultures can't understand a desire so strong to end life that you'd even end your own just to take a few of us out with you."

"*Of course* you don't understand, but then you don't even try to. You don't even desire to understand. You much prefer to just fear us, keep us away, or better yet, under surveillance, you watch us, waiting to catch us, believing we are all going to hurt you. If not now, it's only a matter of time."

"Well, sometimes that suspicion is well founded," said Craig.

"What are you accusing me of?"

"Accusations? No, no, I don't think you understand. The time for accusations came and went. We're way beyond that. We know who you are, we know what you've done, and we even have a good idea why you did it. So, no ma'am, this isn't about accusations. This is about salvation—yours."

"If you really knew everything and already had all the answers, there would be no need for me and I'd already be dead."

Craig was still waiting for intelligence from Scott, having nowhere to possibly take this interrogation until it arrived. The signal for him to come out of the room was a massive relief, as he hoped it meant Scott had something for him.

It was Scott, and he was smiling, so there was good news.

Scott began. "So it's not a lot, but here's a bit of information about where she comes from."

Craig read it over and looked up at his companion with raised eyebrows to indicate how impressed he was. He wanted to say, "Thanks, hon" but instead said, "Thanks, Scott. I can use this now."

Craig walked into the room where Rezeya was waiting and began immediately reading what Scott had discovered so far.

"So, you wanted to know what we know about you. We know that your given name is Rezeya Kashani. You were born in Iran but moved to Afghanistan when you were six years old. After the fall of the Taliban in Afghanistan, many of those responsible for the implementation and execution of the airplane attacks of nine eleven escaped into the mountainous region that creates the border between Afghanistan and Pakistan. We know that the mastermind of that plan, and several other plans that never were executed by Osama bin Laden, was none other than Mohammad Hafizullah Kashani, and we know he is your father!"

Taking advantage of her shell shock, Craig kept at it. "What we also know is that you allocated certain cars to certain dealerships. We know how many cars have been equipped with your group's version of a special option. The reason you are alive is we quickly need to know where the hell you sent those cars. And since you've erased all trace of those cars, you do have value to us alive, for now. Millions of lives are at risk. However, we did suspect you might try something as you did in terms of wiping your hard drive, and before you were alerted to come to the CEO's office a restore point was created by the I.T. department, so it's just a matter of time for us to restore that data."

Kundi smiled. "I'm not half as stupid as you'd like me to be. I wiped all information about those cars after sending to dealers we wanted them to go to."

Craig was angry but suppressed his rage. "You must know nothing is ever totally destroyed in digital; it just takes time to restore. Of course, we don't have time, millions could die. You won't further your cause, in fact you'll cement this society's hatred for Islam. You'll only set your cause back decades."

"You must realize by now I don't have much concern for the lives you are worried about. They are casualties in a war you brought on yourselves. So if you are hoping I'll collapse in a heap of crushing guilt by seeing things through your distorted view of humanity like in your perverted Hollywood interpretation of moral conscience, you're going to be sadly disappointed, little man," said Rezeya in her most belittling tone.

Craig barely even smiled at the insult. This woman's view of the world and of America's role in it, particularly in the Middle East, was subject to such extreme myopia there was clearly no point in arguing about that. Her view was a tenet of her faith.

"I understand you have strong beliefs about how the people of Islam have been treated by the international community, and by America in particular. But one thing I hope you will believe is that I do not have any opinion about how a person worships God, or which name they have for God, or even if they believe in a God at all," Craig explained. "Yes, I know that to you that makes me an infidel, but I don't judge anyone for what they believe in. It is not my place to make such a judgment."

"That's the problem with an infidel, you don't believe in anything, or you believe in the wrong things. There is no honor, no duty to an obligation bigger than yourself, bigger than your country, or beyond your life here," Rezeya spat.

"I'll tell you what I believe and love: *this* life, here, now, you and me. And how precious life is—everyone's. God doesn't need my help with mass murder."

She looked into his eyes with hate.

Craig knew he'd never change this woman's belief. What he did hope to change was her ability to consider that different ideas could co-exist. His was not to argue but rather play to her sense of curiosity, with the hope that she would begin to ask questions—to maybe *try* to understand something else. He needed to plant that seed.

This was all a primer to the bigger goal of driving in a wedge between what she knew to be true and those things she might never have considered. His strategy: to prompt questions in her mind by presenting certain facts he hoped Scott Barton would be successful in digging up. These facts might just be big enough to create a crack of doubt. That's all he needed, a crack in which to drive his wedge—and he could create a chasm.

JUNE 28, 14:05 EDT

Detroit, Michigan

"Focus on the father. He is the same man he has always been. Follow his life day by day back in time and you'll find the story of his daughter." That was the advice Craig received from the director, who then shared it with Scott.

The NSA's not-as-secret-as-they-would-like-to-believe supercomputer had been chewing on the small pieces of information he'd been able to feed it. The director was half right, but it was not the father's past that produced the greatest revelations. They discovered Rezeya's mother was alive and well, living in a quiet suburb of Paris. Rezeya had always been told her mother was dead.

In a twisted, cruel deception, her father had lied to the girl about her mother starting from when Rezeya was six. This lie had a purpose: to manipulate a little girl's psyche and thereby shape her hatred of the West. The deception made it that much easier to press her into service when the time was right, harnessing that carefully cultivated hate to further the cause of Islamic extremism.

Rezeya grew up believing her mother was killed by the Americans, who, she was told, were operating covertly and illegally in Iran, chasing so-called terrorists who were supplying Iraqi subversives with arms, training, and explosives.

In this case, the omission of selected facts lent credence to the tale. It's true that Rezeya's mother was shot during a raid by the Americans, who had grown tired of border crossings into Iraq by Iranians who operated with their government's approval. The shot, though, was not delivered by Americans.

No matter; any and all collateral deaths and injuries were always blamed on the Americans. The state-owned Iranian news made sure. Never mind that the Iranians had been using American-made weapons and artillery for some time in these border conflicts; evidence was rarely needed. Fars News Agency could be relied on to tell the story from the perspective of the Islamic militants.

This particular attack had been covered extensively for a reason. Rezeya's mother was the daughter of a prominent industrialist who owned Iran's most prestigious electrical engineering firm. He was loyal to the Shah and rejected the change to an Islamic Republic. He feared the power given to one man, the Ayatollah. To have an entire country led by one omnipotent Supreme Leader was a terrifying concept, one he feared would lead the nation to isolation from the rest of the world.

Rezeya's grandfather led a small but fierce faction that supported the Shah and opposed those who wanted regime change. Naturally, his business became a target for takeover when the new regime took power—and just as naturally, his death warrant had been signed.

He did manage one thing, though, to keep his daughter safe: marrying her off to a man gaining prominence in the new regime, a man he hated to the core. This was a man whose beliefs of what was best for the country were the polar opposite of his own. At this point, all that mattered was his daughter's life. That was December 14, 1977, two years before the storm.

His deal: he would turn over all his work on the plans he and his company had done on the design of a nuclear reactor in exchange for the safe passage and marriage of his daughter to a man "tight" with the reformist organization.

Rezeya was born less than a year after the marriage, and her grandfather was put to death the next day.

JUNE 28, 16:49 EDT

Detroit, Michigan

Unblinkingly, Scott Barton had been watching the *processing inquiry* message on the terminal screen for the past forty-four minutes, an eternity. His dry eyes and twitching fingers noticed *inquiry complete* but took a second to respond.

Typing in his password yet again, the report began to stream onto the screen. He read quickly, unlike an analyst. There wasn't time. He had to get the meat out of the dry text. There it was on the fourth page, a glimmer of hope, something they might be able to use.

The first good news of this whole damn drama.

Scott called Director Richards and explained what he found. He told him he urgently needed a team in Paris to get to an address on the outskirts of the city and set up a video uplink directly to the Detroit office.

Rushing to the elevator, he snatched the page being printed out. Impatient for the elevator, he began to pace, resisting the urge to take the stairs—which would do him no good, since he lacked access to the underground levels. Craig was going to be elated.

Running down the hall to the interrogation rooms, Scott had to force himself to settle. Getting an investigator out of a room *never* involved rushing in. Instead, a signal of blinking lights is used, visible to the interrogator. Once the signal is seen, the interrogator can then segue departure.

Scott made the signal, then paced. At last, the door opened, and Craig came out. Scott almost didn't recognize him. He seemed to have aged ten years and looked as though he hadn't slept in a week. It broke his heart, but he handed over the page and began to tell Craig the story.

Craig's eyes lit up and he kissed Scott's forehead, not caring what anyone might think. He would have kissed anyone bearing this news. He started back in and Scott stopped him.

"Wait. You look like shit. You're haggard and beat. Let me talk to her."

"Thanks a lot! Great seeing y—" stopping midsentence, he knew Scott was right. "Yeah ... yes, you're right. Besides, she hates my guts; chances are good you'll get further than I will. The stakes are high. This is the biggest crisis we'll ever see—if there is a God," said Craig. "I sure as hell don't believe I am the only person can get her to cooperate."

Scott gripped Craig's shoulder. "Have a seat. Watch me. If you see me messing up, come in. There's no way you can offend me. This isn't my usual thing."

"Yeah, I know you're all about the behind-the-scenes shit, but I have a feeling you are definitely what we need now. A fresh voice and face, and a much more empathetic one at that. And you have a better read on people than anyone I know other than my CIA recruiter, Pecone—at least with me—and I like to think I'm pretty hard to read."

Scott smiled, at the same time terrified with his hand on the door, waiting for the electronic lock to buzz. Once he was in, he saw her at the table, defiant and angry. Instantly, he thought, *She hates me too.*

Something within him told him to smile the biggest, warmest, friendliest smile he could offer. And there it was: a crack, a glimmer of humanity, a slight disarmament of the hostility, tempered still with a solid look of distrust.

She spoke. "And who are you supposed to be? The good cop, I suppose?"

"I'll not pretend that I am any such thing to you, ma'am, but my name is Scott Barton, and there's some information I hope you'll let me share with you about your past. There are a few things you may have been told that are not true."

She hadn't heard anything past the name. She narrowed her eyes with questioning disbelief. "Barton as in President Barton?"

"I am his son, and also an analyst with the National Security Agency, which is why I've come to talk with you."

"*Ummmmph,* like I'd believe anything to come from that den of liars!"

"I know you have to believe that. Your life experiences have given you no other information on which to base your opinions. But can you accept that we do have the most advanced computers in the world? They are capable of searching nearly anything that's ever been accessible to anyone, anywhere, by remote access. Web pages, scanned documents emailed to someone, bank records, vital statistics on births, deaths, marriages, credit applications and reports, tax records, phone usage data, cellphone text messages . . . if anyone has been able to access a piece of information from any computer connected to a phone line or network that has any open communication outside, or has been transmitted by any form of broadcast, we've seen it, cataloged it, and stored it," Scott explained.

"Knowing how you believe everything is yours, I'd not be surprised!" muttered Rezeya.

"Good, so at least you can believe it, while you may begrudge that we do it. This computer can also search a massive clearinghouse of data, based on a visual memory of pictures, names, dates, and many other criteria, with a relational ability that comes as close to 'thinking' as is currently possible with a computer," said Scott.

"Like all Americans, you sound so proud of the things you have access to as a result of the money you have made off the backs of the poor people the world over." The disdain in her voice was venomous.

"I've heard those sentiments before, and while I'd love to talk politics, that's not why I'm here. The point is, we have found your mother. She is very much alive and living a secluded life in a small town south of Paris."

"What do you take me for? I've been taught your tricks since childhood. My father made sure I was aware of your games. The supporters of the Shah killed my mother, with the assistance of your own CIA. I know what happened to her. Using the memory of a pure and good woman to attempt to turn me from the just cause of Allah is pure evil!"

Scott asked with sympathy, "Do you remember her? Her voice, what she looks like? I know you were young and it's been almost forty years, but if you saw her now, would you recognize her?"

Perplexed, her facial expression softened. On the opposite wall, in what she knew to be a one-way window, a video screen came to life with the image of a single woman at a kitchen table in a small apartment with exposed stone walls. Not stone walls as in Iran or the Middle East, but more the type of construction in an older European home or farmhouse. These were small blocks of limestone with varying gaps of thick mortar holding them together, at the same time rustic and classical.

It was a simple and solid wooden table, probably a hundred years old. Seated at the end was a woman, mid-sixties, smiling but sad. The image was crystal clear, with occasional digital artifacts appearing as small blocks here and there. Suddenly the woman's expression changed. She squinted and drew back, then leaned forward, eyes wide, as her hand came to her face, her fingers gently covering her mouth. Then a gasp, a sob.

At once Rezeya saw the woman recognized her. This old woman somewhere on the other end of a satellite feed seemed to know her. Still stubborn, Rezeya told herself an actor could appear to recognize a long-lost daughter and come to tears at will.

"Can she hear me?" Rezeya asked.

Scott faintly raised his eyebrows as the woman responded to the question herself. "Yes, daughter, I can hear you."

Squinting one eye, Rezeya asked the woman why she thought she was her daughter.

"Simple. When I saw you, I thought I was looking in a mirror that could take thirty years off my face."

It was an answer from a simple woman, not from a script. The beginnings of belief were invading her skepticism. Far from convinced, Rezeya crossed her arms in that way typical of blocking the advance of someone into her personal space. "Where have you been? You were killed."

"No, my dear, I escaped. It's a very long story, but I ran from your father. I tried to take you; he found us. He nearly killed me and left me for dead. My mother and brothers found me and nursed me for months. Your father left, with you, but we knew he'd be back. He sent word that you'd been sent away, I'd never find you, and that he was going to come and finish what he started with me. I fled and eventually settled in France, where I blended in with the Algerians. I tried to keep tabs on you, but you had literally disappeared off the face of the earth. Your father eventually did as well. I knew it was the work of the new leaders of Iran. I also knew going back would be a death sentence. All I could do was pray—and I did pray, four times a day—that one day, Allah would bring you back to me."

The older woman reached across the table, pulling a picture in a frame into the field of vision of the camera. As it came into focus, it was now Rezeya's turn to go through the difficult recognition, remembering the scene in the picture as though it were yesterday. It was her, her mother, and her father at the shore of the Caspian Sea during a time when Iran was much more liberal, and people went to the shore to play in the water and sand and eat falafel and caviar from vendors. It was a good memory of a peaceful time, a time when they were a family. Even then, though, her father's expression was cold, with a determined look in his eyes.

Though teary, Rezeya wasn't yet convinced this woman was her mother—and even if she were, did it matter? Would it change anything? Would the passion her father held for the "cause" be lessened in meaning and importance to her just because she had been taken from her mother and her life molded into that of a soldier of Allah? Yet, there remained too many questions, shaking the foundation of her identity. She was always her father's daughter; but what if she was also her mother's? Could she be both? That didn't seem possible.

"Why does my father appear angry in the picture, when it seemed like we were so happy?"

"Even though I never felt love for your father—ours was an arranged marriage— I was told my father set it up to protect me; even so, there were times I thought he was a good man. But he was always hard-hearted. He'd look at the way people were enjoying themselves, at the beach, for instance, with a judgmental scorn.

"I know that your father is wrong, the West is not godless. They allow me to live." At once she looked incredibly sad.

"The men who came here tonight," she continued, "told me nothing about what is happening, only that they have found you and that you are in trouble. Listen to me, my daughter. I have been praying to find you ever since I lost you. I welcomed these men into my home because they told me they had found you. In my eyes, they are messengers from Allah. He sent them and now I pray to hold you in my arms again."

Rezeya was not broken, her hardness was softening, but her devotion to the cause, to her father, was too entrenched. She had found her mother but realized a reunion was a possibility she herself had destroyed. Surely these people would kill her when this was over. She would never see her mother again.

"*Mother*, I don't see a future where that is possible. I can't undo the things I have done, and I am convinced these people will kill me, either secretly or by conviction through a trial."

Rezeya's mother reacted the way only a mother can when her offspring is threatened. "Who's in charge there? I want to see your face!"

Scott Barton walked into view of the camera off to the side of Rezeya. "Do you know who I am, Mrs. Kundi?"

Her eyes expressed a smile. "Yes, of course, I know you are the president's son. Though I may not like everything your father has done, he's a better man than some others who've sat in his office."

"Thank you, Mrs. Kundi. I'll let him know, and I hope you understand that he's not always able to do all things the way he'd like to."

Mrs. Kundi looked down, slightly nodding. "Then I like him even more. Some men push their will through regardless of the thoughts or concerns of those around them."

"Yes ... but if I may, Mrs. Kundi, I must press on. Time is not on our side."

"I understand, sir, but you can't go yet. I want you to promise me that if my daughter helps you now, her life will be spared!" For emphasis, she pounded the table with her fist. *"Promise me!"*

Scott was in a spot. He wasn't sure he could make that promise—but decided to anyway, knowing the directive of this mission and that his dad would back him up.

"Mrs. Kundi ... if your daughter cooperates with us *immediately* and helps us stop this catastrophe ... I promise she will live."

"Rezeya, you must trust this man. I think he is the best hope we have of ever seeing each other again."

Rezeya was softening, feeling the true pain of those words. She wasn't sure that would happen no matter what she did.

"Thank you, Mrs. Kundi. The men who are with you will be staying with you until we can get you to a safe place."

The careworn though respectful motion of her nod was of a kind that said, *I believe you and trust you. I can only hope you will do right by me.*

Scott read it perfectly and returned the same wordless commitment. The high-tech digital screen went to a white line in the center, followed by a bright white dot and then nothing. Rezeya was there reflected with glassy eyes, seated at a table with the president's son standing over her.

Scott gently touched her shoulder. She didn't flinch, and he sensed that she didn't feel affronted.

"Rezeya, I promise you, if you cooperate, and help us all you can, you and your mother will be together. At least she will be allowed to visit you. But that is all I can promise at this point."

The skeptical look returned. "You will let me live?" It was more a statement of disbelief. "I mean, even if I help you in every way I can, and trust me if I agree to help you it will be with my full capacity, but will I live if even we fail?"

Now it was Scott's turn to look puzzled. "Fail?"

Suddenly it dawned on her that maybe they had no idea of the scope of this operation. Just maybe she had a bigger bargaining chip than she thought.

"What do you know?" she asked.

"Not enough. Well, let me be precise. We know they've put nuclear bombs in cars. We found one in the San Francisco Bay Area. We know there are seven more out there. But, we don't know you know where they were sent."

She appreciated both his honesty and that he said *they've*, meaning she was no longer part of *them*, at least for the immediate future. How long that would remain the case was yet to be seen.

"So, you know how many?"

"Not with the certainty we would prefer, but we know a transport truck in Korea holds eight cars, so we assume that's the maximum number, and we have statements from the driver that there are eight bombs. The validity of that assertion, though, is suspect. We find it difficult to believe their resources were capable of equipping eight cars with a nuclear device."

Rezeya didn't want to gloat; but, after all, they did manage to do something the West never thought they could.

"This is the first point at which I will help you. There were eight devices; however, with the failure of the one you discovered, now there are seven. They are positioned in cities of strategic military interest or in those that will produce the most civilian devastation. In some cases, both."

Scott listened. He needed to know so much more about this operation: the motives, the players, the resources, how they were able to turn Secretary Bonner. Still, he was extremely doubtful. The problem with "turned" informants is that they're notoriously unreliable, if not downright liars. Getting enough weapons-grade plutonium is not something you pick up at your local munitions supplier. The rest—building the weapons, electronics, igniters, and so on—he thought possible; but to trust her, that was the biggest problem.

"Do you expect me to believe you were able to obtain enough weapons-grade plutonium to build eight nuclear devices with enough force to destroy or seriously damage an entire city?"

"If you didn't believe me, I don't think we'd be here."

"OK, so then ... how?"

"You don't think I know all the details of the operation, do you? We know what we need to know to accomplish our mission."

"But you know there is a nuclear bomb in each of the cars?"

"Yes, that was necessary for them to make clear, to impress on me the importance of my mission."

"And your mission specifically?"

"To make sure the cars with the VIN numbers I was provided got to the dealerships that were strategically selected."

"What cities?"

"San Francisco."

"We already know about San Francisco. You'll need to be a lot more forthcoming if you expect to ever see the light of day again," said Scott firmly, though he knew she'd not likely fully cooperate.

"I have no idea what you are promising for me to be more ... *forthcoming*, as you call it. What is the point? You now know where the cars were allocated; you are, I'm sure, dispatching people to those dealerships as I sit here. The information I've received about my mother, and my father's deceptions, is confusing, still new to me, still *unbelievable*."

"Ms. Kundi, I know what you've learned in the past few hours is a lot to absorb. I know your life was dedicated to this cause from before you were even old enough to speak. You seem like a very logical person, someone who greatly values pragmatism. Would you agree?"

Rezeya took several minutes to ponder Scott's question. Scott, for his part, well understood the value of patient silence.

After a long breath, Rezeya responded with equal formality. "Mr. Barton, pragmatically, you must know that a video conference with my resurrected mother couldn't possibly alter what I believe. That includes fully accepting that she is my mother."

Scott took note of the formality and could see it represented a barrier. He placed his hand on his chest and said genuinely, "Please call me Scott."

Rezeya, recognizing his open body language and hearing the gentle sincerity in his voice, acknowledged him with a long blink and continued, "If I am to be completely honest with myself, I admit living in this country has changed me. I have seen charity and selflessness, but also intolerance, religious hatred, racism ..." her tone grew dark.

Scott thought better than to pursue this train of thought. *Join with her,* he considered, *then move to the subject of the plans.* "This is true," he admitted, "I too have seen it here. We're humans, and humans have all of those feelings. It can be so destructive. I've also seen extraordinary compassion—once, I'll never forget, in Iran ..."

Rezeya's eyes lit up.

Scott knew that while Rezeya was unlikely to break, it might be possible to continue as though they were just having a philosophical conversation. "The deepest connection of feeling can come from the most unlikely places."

Rezeya looked lost in her own musings, as though grappling with something. Scott spoke.

"We know cars were sent to San Francisco, San Diego, Las Vegas, Washington, D.C., Fayetteville, Newark, Denver and Albuquerque; after all," he continued, "since we already know this, you don't betray anyone by confirming the information."

Rezeya looked up and squinted at him, indicating some—but not total— suspicion. She still had doubts, he could see. "I suppose you're also going to suggest that I in some way can help myself while not being responsible for bringing our plan to a failure?"

Scott picked up what he hoped was the beginning of a negotiation.

"Yes, the plot has already failed, we know where the cars were sent, we have to find them on our own, we know that once they went to the dealerships you'd not know what happened with them afterward."

"I am curious how you found the cities?"

"I'd like to say it was simple, that we recovered the data, but it was old-fashioned investigative work. We had the VINs from the cars that were on the same truck with the one we found in San Francisco. From there, we had to contact the DMV for each state to see if they had any registration records for those VINs."

Rezeya knew the states didn't share this information with any data clearinghouse, so she was impressed. "That was clever, though I'm sure you had some states that were not very cooperative," she said, barely able to suppress a grin. "But you do need something, information of some kind, or I would not be here."

"Yes, and I have been authorized to offer you life, in a federal prison, with visitation rights, with the provision of supervised probation in fifteen years."

"Is that all?"

Scott knew it didn't sound great, so he explained the alternative. "You're an American citizen, you will be tried for treason, I am a hundred percent confident you will be found guilty; treason carries the death penalty. Also, you could be held at Guantanamo indefinitely as an enemy combatant, never to see anyone again. I hope you can see it's actually very generous. I would ask you to ponder, what would the leaders of your country offer?"

Rezeya, realizing her negotiating position wasn't a strong one, still wanted some element of winning something. "I'll accept, but I want it in writing with your father's signature," she declared.

"I can make that happen, but can we keep talking while we wait for that?"

"We can talk for an hour, then I want to see the papers before we continue," she said.

Scott was impressed with her savviness and decided to dive right in.

"So, I'll ask again, are those cities correct?"

"Yes, those are the cities."

"Ms. Kundi, I would appreciate your being open and forthcoming with your answers. Are there any other cities?"

Rezeya, nodding that she understood and agreed, said, "No. There were eight cars and eight cities."

"OK, so I can understand, some locations, Washington, D.C., for example, are obvious; even Las Vegas, though not a typical target. But why Fayetteville and Albuquerque, and why Newark over New York?"

"I don't know. I didn't choose the cities and was ordered to find a dealership near those cities where the car could be delivered. In the case of Fayetteville and San Diego, I know the cars were intended to go into service with a rental car company; but as for *why* those places, I can only tell you that I overheard discussion of cities being selected for either their financial or social impact: where a bomb would generate the most public spectacle, which is, I am sure, why Las Vegas was selected. The other thing I can guess is that there is a military target nearby that is of importance in some way."

JUNE 28, 16:49 EDT

Detroit, Michigan

Fayetteville, North Carolina, is one of those places in the world that wouldn't exist if it weren't for a large industrial complex right on the edge of its borders. Some of those cities have their destiny anchored to a large corporation. Like Dearborn, Michigan, and Ford Motor Company; or Akron, Ohio, and Goodyear Rubber. Industry isn't always business. Oftentimes it's also government. On the northern border of Fayetteville lies one of America's largest military installations. Technically, it is two installations, the army's Fort Bragg and Pope Air Force Base, which sits adjacent to Fort Bragg.

By East Coast standards, Fort Bragg is a relatively modern installation, established as a camp in 1918 and later, as it became a permanent installation, renamed Fort Bragg in 1922. In a stroke of irony, the base was named after North Carolina–born and raised Confederate army general Braxton Bragg—who, of course, fought against the United States in the Civil War.

In terms of strategic importance, Fort Bragg would not be on the top of the list for many, but since the beginning of the wars in Afghanistan and Iraq, Fort Bragg had seen its population and scope increase. The headquarters of the XVIII Airborne Corps was located there, which had deployed in both conflicts.

Also, a division of the U.S. Army Special Operations Command, with the 4th Psychological Operations Group (its subordinate unit), is based at Fort Bragg. The mission of this group: to disseminate information in hostile areas that will motivate the people of those areas to desire the fundamentals of freedom and independence from a usually totalitarian leadership.

A terrorist weapon was placed near this base.

What Pope AFB has that made it a desired target resides several stories underground, below in an innocuous red brick building. While meant to appear ordinary, what surrounded the building was anything but. In addition to the antenna array above was fencing topped by concertino wire. Armed guards manned a gate with a steel barrier.

Inside, the façade continues. Dull, institutional square tiles made of some kind of synthetic material cover the floors—and are likely to be found completely intact and polished by future archaeologists. Four-inch-high rubberized baseboard moldings and cinderblock walls have been painted white gray in so many high-gloss layers it's hard to know that indeed they are cinderblock.

Down the hall are steel doors in a color neither brown nor tan, with small rectangular windows containing square-patterned wire mesh inside the glass, and small signs carved in brown plastic with yellowed block lettering that used to be white. Consistent with the military's penchant for acronyms, the signs read only AFI 1-A, AFI 1-B, and so on, meaning Air Force Intelligence floor 1 room A or room B, et cetera. In the middle of the hall, a door is marked AFI STA SECURITY CLEARANCE REQUIRED.

A card is swiped through the reader, the door's electronic magnetic lock releases, and the door opens as any other door. Six feet ahead is another door with another card reader. The point of this arrangement is that the first door locks before one can physically reach the retina and fingerprint scanner for the second door. If an unauthorized person were to get past the first door, that person would be locked in; there's no going back. Beyond the second door are two armed sentries wearing Kevlar–carbon fiber full body protection.

Once past these sentries, more scans are required to call the elevator directly ahead. Card, retina, fingerprint. A password is entered and the controls become active. Once inside the elevator, the floor determines the weight of the occupant. If it matches within a range of 10 percent of the person's known weight (on file, for security clearance), the buttons to the floors allowed per specific clearance light up for selection.

Only one person at a time can ride, with no allowance for guests. (Guests, if any were to visit this facility, would have to be granted a security card and have a retina and fingerprint ID entered into the security system's database.) The levels on the elevator's selection pad are S4-S17 (subterranean level four through seventeen). When the elevator is exited, another armed sentry appears—with gun drawn and ready to fire. Once identity and status are confirmed, the person is allowed to pass. It has been deemed that person belongs here.

This facility is dedicated to Air Force Intelligence counterterrorism operations and special intelligence command for the Middle East. All that the United States and most of her allies knows about the Middle East or terrorism has come though this facility. It had been Osama bin Laden's number-one target, and it remains a target in his memory.

Bin Laden hated the place that kept watch on him, that prevented his movements in open air, and that forced him to never see the light of day. He had been a prisoner for more than a decade. This place tried to persuade his devout followers that their futures would be richer, fuller, and filled with more content if they rejected the principles and policies of their extremist faction and accept the liberal doctrine of the West. In bin Laden's mind, this place was evil, and Allah had told him it must be destroyed.

JUNE 28, 20:25 EDT

Detroit, Michigan

Rezeya had grown suspicious again. While seeing and hearing her mother in real time was powerful evidence that she was alive, she was bothered by something the president's charming son had said. The intelligence capabilities of this country were astonishing, the supercomputers proved it. How hard would it be then for such a country to fake a live video conference?

While she'd been moved to a more comfortable place, less sterile and with more of an American living room feel, she knew that her every move and look around, every visible emotion, was monitored.

Barton had been gone maybe twenty minutes, barely long enough for her to get settled in her new surroundings. Choosing one of the overstuffed lounge chairs, she had just taken a sip of cool water when Scott Barton along with Craig Stout arrived.

"Is this more comfortable?" Scott asked.

"Well, yes, of course. If nothing else, the lighting is less harsh and I can feel more relaxed, but I'll be honest with you, I still don't know if I can trust you." She said this to Scott, directing her eyes to Craig.

Scott put his arm around Craig's shoulder as a show of trust, as a way to say *he's with me.*

Rezeya, sensing the underlying feelings, said, "I do not approve of homosexuality, but I have heard the rumors of you for years, and I've worked with other homosexuals—who I've found to be helpful and generous and kindhearted ... a sign of weakness to many, but something I've learned to appreciate in a way."

Scott said nothing more than "Yes ma'am."

"Once I help you, and you have all you think you need from me, will I just be put to the wolves, either your wolves or those from my past?" she asked.

Scott studied her. Her eyes told him that she hadn't lied, but she needed reassurance. "You're right to worry about the wolves. More yours, I'd say, than ours. Maybe this will help." Scott handed her a document with the presidential seal emblazoned at the top.

Rezeya took the document and read it. "Thank you," she said, clearly deep in thought.

"Is there something else?" asked Scott, disturbed by a lingering sense of reluctance.

"I want to see my mother in person."

This time it was Craig who responded, hoping to gain some measure of trust. "She's in flight already, in business class, Air France, a flight we held for almost an hour so she could make it. I'd considered a military flight but didn't think she'd be too comfortable ... she'll be here in about seven hours. I promise."

"So, now you expect me to tell you more? You want me to trust you as well?" Her eyes were boring a hole in Craig.

He looked straight back into her eyes and said, "I need you to trust me. I need you to help me, so we can limit the impact of this. This benefits your people, too. You know our leaders would have no choice but to retaliate. Can you even image what that would be like? If what you have told us and continue to tell us is true, you are the only hope for millions of people, not just Americans. I want you to know, if you help us, if you cooperate, you will never want for anything again. You and your mother will be taken care of for the rest of your natural lives, granted for at least the next fifteen years, yours will be in a federal prison, I'm sorry, but there is just no way around that."

"Thank you, Mr. Stout, for your honesty."

"The most peaceful time I remember is the summer with my parents at the Caspian Sea. Oh, what a beautiful place that was." Her melancholy made it clear that she wanted to live a life of her choosing, not one chosen for her.

"Ms. Kundi, that place no longer exists, you can only ever be there in your memories," Scott said. "Since the Ayatollah ordered the thousands of Cyprus trees cut down—that once lined the beautiful shore—I'm not at all sure the present-day sight would be anything close to what's in your mind. So maybe it's for the best."

"Why did he do that?"

"It seems he built a massive vacation complex there and felt the trees obstructed the view of the sea."

"Damned fool."

It was a start.

JUNE 28, 21:05 EDT

Detroit, Michigan

"Which car do you want to know about first?" asked Rezeya.

Since they already had one in San Francisco, Scott wondered where that one was intended to go; asking about it perhaps would ease her into giving up the other cars.

"The one we found near San Francisco—where was it supposed to go?"

She gave him a troubled look. Yes, she'd agreed to help, but this was it. This was the moment she would be a traitor to her past and all that defined her life.

"Very well. I will tell you as I have promised. Now I hope and pray you are good on your word as well," said Rezeya. "There were several cars on the same ship that arrived at that port of entry. From the reports I'd received at work, I'd noticed one car that was going to be delayed to its destination due to a mechanical failure. This is also when I knew I might have to run.

"That car was supposed to go to Albuquerque; more specifically, to Espanola, New Mexico. It was being delivered to Henry Valencia Chevrolet, where it had been ordered by a customer in nearby Los Alamos. But with the mechanical failure, I reallocated another car for that destination, sparing the city of San Francisco as one of the targets."

"A customer?" asked Craig, ignoring her comment about sparing San Francisco. He was glad that was one less target, but he wanted to focus on the others.

"One of ours. You call them sleepers, of course. His mission was to get a menial job at the National Laboratories in Los Alamos, drive the car to work one night and fulfill its mission."

"Its mission being to destroy the National Laboratories along with himself?" Craig asked with no small amount of disgust, immediately regretting his interjection. He privately resolved for Scott to continue without his asides.

"Much of the world looks at the facility where the atomic bomb was developed with disdain and disgust."

"That's true—and that early end to that war saved hundreds of thousands of lives, all around." Craig could hear himself arguing.

"Maybe the world's issue with this has to do with the staggering number of nonmilitary causalities—terrorism, by your own standards. It was the best example used by our early leaders to justify our means, that the world had changed, that standard military action was less than efficient," Rezeya replied.

"That's a hell of a reach in logic," said Craig, digging himself in deeper against his own rule.

"Setting aside your own dogma," she challenged, "how is a terrorist act defined?"

"Number one, it's an act performed by an individual or a group not considered to be a sovereign government. Number two, it tends to focus on civilian targets to accomplish its primary intent—that is, to create terror and anarchy so the government must bow to the demands of the terrorists," Craig responded.

"Just so: the intent behind Hiroshima and Nagasaki, to instill the fear of further reprisals and obtain unconditional surrender."

"You can't ignore it was done by a sovereign nation at a time of war."

"Ah, but there are those who believe the Islamic Nation has sovereign rights and is at war with America."

Craig took that in. It was a perspective he couldn't outright reject.

"OK, but the question remains: Is the dispute of Islam with America or the West? Or is it just with anyone who doesn't subscribe to the same beliefs? That's the problem, and I think you're beginning to see it yourself," Craig felt he had to point out, despite the risk that she might not talk.

"Yes ... perhaps so," acknowledged Rezeya.

JUNE 28, 22:43 EDT

Detroit, Michigan

"I'm still not supportive of the idea of bringing a terrorist's mother here in order to appease her," grumbled Craig, as he and Scott took a moment outside of the area where Rezeya was being held. "No. No, I don't like it one fucking bit!"

"Would you freaking calm down?" Scott shot back. "There's one way and one way only you are going to get what you need to minimize this disaster!" Craig's concern showed. He noticed Scott said *minimize* and not *eliminate*.

Scott continued. "That's right, I said *minimize*. The reality is very doubtful that we will be able to locate all the devices before they are programmed to detonate."

"So we are doomed to failure?"

"Only by the insane all-or-nothing standards of fail-succeed measure used in the CIA and FBI. Everything is not simply black and white. The measurement of success here is that we can save millions of lives, even if there's no way to make this quietly go away."

Craig was still grumbling. "I'd prefer the *quietly go away, no one ever needs to know, and those responsible are quietly dropped off a cliff somewhere* option, not reunite them with their mommies to live happily ever after."

"Grow up! You know damn well these women will never ever have a moment of bliss. They'll be hiding from their accomplices for the rest of their lives, however short that may be."

That actually seemed to appease Craig to some degree, and Scott asked himself again for the hundredth time, *How the hell can I love this guy?*

"In a nutshell, there are seven atomic bombs positioned around the country all set by the atomic clock in Boulder, Colorado. At twelve o'clock midnight on July fourth, they will detonate."

"For a guy who is much more emotional than I'll ever be, you sure didn't sugarcoat that one. Why don't we just turn off the atomic clock or at least its transmission?" asked Craig.

"Yeah, I thought of that, but the bombs were activated when they approached their respective ports and came into the range of the clock's transmission. Once the time is set to the clock, the bombs are dependent upon their own quartz movements to detonate. The designers are OK with a few seconds between detonations due to minor clock inaccuracies but wanted make sure it wasn't a few minutes or hours."

"Jesus," followed by a long pause, was all Craig could manage. Once he had absorbed it, the magnitude of scale, his mind went into autopilot crisis response mode.

"OK, seven bombs. I take it we'll have to triage them?" asked Craig.

"Ideally, but we are still getting details about the cars those bombs are contained in, where they are right now, as opposed to the dealership they were shipped to. Our source has given us the dealerships, the date and time of the arrival of the cars, and in cases where the cars have been sold to customers, all the details of that transaction."

"Sold? Wait a minute, you mean there are unsuspecting customers out there with atomic bombs in their car they know nothing about?"

"No, the buyers are actually sleepers. They got a menial job at some strategic location, as a janitor, say, or a night maintenance person at a place like the Naval Base San Diego or the National Laboratories. Or maybe the car was put into rental service near a military base like Fort Bragg with the hope some enlisted grunt would need wheels."

Craig paled.

"I've surmised," Scott continued, "based on where the cars were delivered to. Most of the sleepers' actual jobs and locations weren't known to our source. Typical smart 'need to know' organization. Albuquerque, though, we have Rezeya to thank for: she did know it was ordered by an employee of the National Laboratories. She didn't have this knowledge from her organization, but rather from the dealer who'd ordered the car, and called to follow up on its ETA."

"How'd the dealer know? From a credit application? I can't imagine these people were that dumb!"

"No, they aren't, unfortunately for us. It was pure luck, since it was a cash deal; but at some point, the dealer saw the buyer's employee ID tag clipped to his belt. He used the information to push the shipping of the car, telling Rezeya, *We gotta do our best for the 'boys' working at the labs.* When the car had been delayed in San Francisco—because it was the one we found—she reallocated the car intended for San Francisco, as she felt Los Alamos was a more important target."

Craig began to look as though he'd underestimated the turning of Rezeya.

"Humph, I'll be damned. She seems to be willing to give it all up. You still a hundred percent your balls on the line kind of sure she's really on our side now?"

"I'm sure, but I'd appreciate you keeping my balls out of it."

"So ... I need to find seven cars, with only color, make, model, year and VIN? And that those cars could be just about anywhere within about a hundred miles of a dealership's location?"

"Yeah. You'll need plenty of help you can trust."

"Trust? Fuck are you kidding me? The only person I trust with this is me!" He instantly regretted saying it as the words left his lips.

"Unless you can make seven clones of your narcissistic ass in the next ten minutes, I don't see you have a much of a choice," said Scott, frustrated with Craig's most annoying trait of overconfidence.

Craig exhaled a long breath, then bluntly asked, "What are the damn locations?"

JUNE 29, 16:15 EDT

East Coast, United States

The largest multi-enforcement operation in the free world began on June 29 at 14:15 Mountain Daylight Time. Given that the atomic clock is in Boulder, Colorado, it was thought that the clocks would all be set to Mountain Time, that the terrorists wanted the bombs to go off simultaneously.

Analysis of the San Francisco bomb's detonator revealed there was a GPS locator as well, indicating the intent was to detonate the bombs over a three-hour period. Clearly, they wanted to maximize the terror as much as possible. The agony and anxiety created while a nation is forced to anticipate the next explosion exploits the terror most effectively.

The worst part of this was that the bombs on the East Coast would be the first to explode by three hours. The population density of the East Coast presented additional challenges in finding the cars and at the same time evacuating the cities.

In Washington, D.C., and Newark, New Jersey, the FBI would head up the search. The local police departments would be enlisted but their instructions would be limited to locating and holding the car, then immediately contacting the FBI. The FBI's counterterrorism unit had instructions for disarming the device based on the study of the bomb found in San Francisco.

Fearing panic, local politicians were slow to consider mass evacuations of their communities. As a result, an unprecedented order came from the White House, based solely on information from Craig and Scott. The president—against the judgment of his advisors—decided the consequences of not evacuating far outweighed the political risks of ordering an evacuation and being wrong. He gave very little weight to what people might think when the potential for loss of life was so great.

Evacuations would begin based on anticipated difficulty. Newark and New York would begin evacuation procedures at 8 A.M. on July 2. This would balance the interests in delaying as long as possible in hope the car would be found, thereby negating the necessity of evacuation and the need to remove people from harm's way. All other cities would have a twenty-four-hour deadline.

The governors of New Jersey, Virginia, Maryland, and New York, due to their proximity to Newark and Washington, D.C., were informed by President Barton himself. They were ordered to mobilize their National Guard units. All traffic was to be reverse flow, leaving Newark and all communities in a twenty-mile radius. This of course included the 14 million people in all five boroughs of New York City, many of whom didn't have a car.

New York City had every imaginable mode of transportation at its disposal. The trick was directing the masses of people in such a way that one method wasn't underutilized while another method had more people than it could accommodate in the given time.

After the embarrassing crisis in New Orleans during Hurricane Katrina, every major U.S. city began the process of reworking evacuation measures. Unfortunately, as is always the case with the public, the vast majority never listens.

How well would they follow the plan? That is precisely the question authorities faced starting in New York City. Every addressable citizen had been given instructions on where to proceed in case of a mass evacuation. Some were told to go to the airport, some to the ferry ports, others to the train stations, yet others to the bus authority; and, of course, many would be using the subways to get to those locations. Come the time of the actual order, though, would any of them remember where they were supposed to go? Or worse, would they simply ignore the instructions, choosing instead the method they preferred? The answer, well, they were about to find out.

JUNE 30, 10:40 MDT

Los Alamos, New Mexico

Only antigovernment wackos in New Mexico became an issue to get out of danger's way. This area of the country had always drawn people eager to buy into just about every crackpot theory that involves a conspiracy, from Big Brother to the deep state and worse. Not only do they exist, according to believers these entities are out to control, deceive, and otherwise screw over the common man at every turn. They remain convinced that if the government says to do something, it is in your best interest to do the exact opposite.

Not coincidentally, this isn't a densely populated part of the country, a fact not lost on Craig. Also, the likelihood of finding a brand-new import car in the desert is far greater than in the greater metropolitan area.

Even though the investigation stage had ended, Craig was still charged with heading up every aspect of this mission by the president himself. "I don't give a shit about the chain of command right now. I need someone I know can produce results, someone I can trust to ride asses and take no shit—no fucking pun intended. You tell anyone who dares to ask, they can follow your orders or resign, and they can call my office to confirm," is what he'd said.

Craig had pointed out he'd been at this for almost six days now with very little sleep and was nearing his physical and mental limits. He'd asked the president if someone fresher wouldn't be more capable. The president's mumbled answer was something to the effect that he'd rather have him, as tired and weary as he was, than someone he didn't emphatically trust, especially while the betrayal of Secretary Bonner was still a stinging wound. "The very fact you are still objective enough to see your limitations is exactly why I need you in there and not some renegade cowboy general."

Craig had learned from Rezeya the general location for every car. That was critical, of course, but not knowing precise location was a problem. Even worse, while Rezeya had information about both the dealership and when a sleeper was used to take over the car, she had no idea what the sleepers' orders were or where they would drive or park the car to strike. She didn't even know what the intended targets were. He still marveled at the effectiveness in which Scott had been able to turn her, even though he still bristled at the thought she'd escaped prosecution to the fullest extent of the law.

The team arrived at the National Labs in full force, with twenty desert-camouflaged Humvees, six of which had center-mounted gun turrets, six black FBI Chevy Suburbans, among which was the FBI's local office bomb squad, and several state and local police cars. Like a choreographed ballet, the Humvees took position at every entry/exit point of the facility while unmarked black FBI vehicles sped in: a one-second delay live satellite image on their navigation system showed the location of the car in the civilian employee parking lot.

Bombs can be detonated in any number of ways. The complexity of the process can vary exponentially, depending on how the bomb is armed and the trigger (or triggers) to detonation. The team in this case had a working knowledge of the bomb's design, thanks to the forensic analysis of the one discovered at the Benicia, CA, port. They knew in advance how these bombs would be armed, and that they had only one trigger to detonate. Knowing there were no trip wires that would deploy the bomb by breaking in, the bomb squad unceremoniously smashed the car's rear windows, pulled out the rear seat cushion, and began the process of defusing the bomb using the information provided by the bomb disposal team in San Francisco. Since the detonation was solely by an internal clock set to detonate precisely at 12:01 July 4, there was no risk in cutting the power supply wires to the bomb. Fortunately, the bomb makers did not have a failsafe, since they didn't assume any bombs would ever be discovered. Typically, a failsafe might be as simple as any wire cut, automatically detonating the bomb. This oversight was a rare lucky break to this horrible turn of events. Within twenty minutes, the danger was nullified.

The other FBI personnel were now in the maintenance building looking for the proud owner of the newly dismantled little red car in the parking lot.

The thirty-eight-year-old Caucasian man, Benjamin Richards, would go to his high-security federal penitentiary cell a year later following his prosecution. He would continue to deny he had any knowledge the car was a delivery device for a nuclear bomb. He would claim to his last day that he was a victim of an overzealous government, that he innocently bought the car from the local dealership, never knowing its ultimate purpose. His denials fell on deaf ears.

JULY 2

Various target cities, United States

A t Fort Bragg, North Carolina, and San Diego, California, the tactical response teams proceeded with nearly the exact same sequence of events as their actions in New Mexico.

The one thing they all had in common was that the primary target was either within a military facility or so closely associated with one that using a satellite to search for the small cars was relatively easy. As a target, the Naval Base San Diego, near downtown San Diego, was one of the worst-case scenarios for those charged with protection of the homeland. It is both a valuable military target and one where a large number of civilian fatalities likely would occur.

When the FBI's request came in to close Interstate 5 at Interstate 805 connector on the north and at the Mexican border on the south, there was initial resistance from local authorities. Yet when it was made clear that if the bomb car wasn't located, traffic between the Los Angeles basin and San Diego would be diverted to Interstate 15 farther inland, the plan was immediately implemented. The evacuation of North San Diego County would be directed to the east, out into the desert communities and on to Palm Springs or even as far as Arizona, if necessary.

While South Orange County would be evacuated to the north, residents were encouraged to travel as far north as possible while avoiding Interstate 15, which would be used to clear Las Vegas.

In the meantime, Scott was using his father's name to re-aim every military and spy satellite onto areas they knew to be targets. The paranoia of the country's intelligence services ramped up into high gear. Director Sessions from the FBI was bitching about the possibility that the plan was to divert America's attention away from the real threat. He was silenced by President Barton, who in a very short phone call made it clear they weren't going to play second-guessing games. They knew these bombs were real, they'd seen one and taken it apart. This was America's first priority and, for the time being, its single security mission. Barton ended the conversation by letting Sessions know that as far as he was concerned, the director's accusations were those of a man whose pride had been wounded by having the CIA take the lead on the investigation from the beginning. If the director continued on this course, he'd be charged with treason and obstruction of justice.

A digital image of the top of a Chevrolet Spark was programmed into the NSA's visual mapping and recognition software. Human eyes would never be able to discern the subtle differences in a car from the top. Even a veteran car designer would struggle to identify his own design when seeing it from that perspective. The system worked flawlessly, thanks to the fact that the Spark is not a common car. The thing was never a hot seller, even in the days when customers were flocking to fuel-sipping cars during the gas price drive up. The Spark sat unsold on car dealership lots.

They found the cars in San Diego, North Carolina, and New Mexico, and thought they knew the location of the one in Colorado.

JULY 2, 11:00 EDT

Broadcast from an undisclosed location

There was no attempt to make President Barton's address warm and friendly. He was not seated in a cozy living room with a crackling fire in the background to project a sense of calm and ease. Some of his advisors had wanted exactly that, but he did not feel that was appropriate.

The broadcast clearly took place in a bunker, for all to see. He told the American people he had taken cover and had ordered the entire cabinet, House of Representatives and Senate to do the same.

"My fellow Americans, as your president, I am charged with the task of telling you there is a credible threat to three of our great cities. This threat has the capacity to cause extreme devastation to New York City, Washington, D.C., and Las Vegas.

"This is not a guess or a rumor. It is conclusive, with one hundred percent certainty. These cities are in grave danger. We have obtained irrefutable evidence, some of which can and will only be released long after these next few days have ended. During the past ten days, our intelligence and military service agencies uncovered this threat and have already eliminated a similar danger from several other cities. Based on the physical evidence we recovered in those cities, we know the threat is genuine. For the last three cities, we have run out of time, and now must completely evacuate them.

"A mandatory evacuation order, organized by state and local authorities, is in effect for the cities of New York, Washington, D.C., and Las Vegas. The evacuation of the New York metropolitan area began early this morning. It is imperative that anyone not in one of these cities remain in their homes, stay off the roads as much as possible, and keep the phone lines clear for emergency use.

"I have ordered all airlines to cease scheduled operations and stage their largest aircraft to assist in the evacuations. Buses and trains also have been routed so as to move as many people as possible and to ease the burden on highways. Every American's cooperation is necessary and expected. As Pearl Harbor was the event that defined a generation, this will be the defining moment of this generation."

The president's message was loud and clear. "Our actions in this time of crisis will define us. We all must find ways to be part of the solution, and not add to the problem. God bless and keep us all!"

People's eyes were steadfastly fixed to TV screens. There was no chatter or discussion, just unwavering shock and horror. It was like watching a train wreck compounded by a factor of ten. You couldn't move. No matter how much you wanted to look away, you couldn't.

JULY 2, 16:30 EDT

New York City

I n New York City, the evacuation had been in progress for close to eight hours. There was a massive law enforcement presence at every exit point of the city. If you were driving your own car and could take more passengers, strangers were put into your vehicle. Everyone was searched for weapons. The entire country was under martial law by executive order of the president.

The ferry ports were swarmed with people, and ferries were coming from every possible nearby city. They were taking people mostly up the Hudson River to points deemed far enough north, or traveling the East River and into the Atlantic to drop people in Connecticut or Rhode Island.

The New York Port Authority Bus Terminal on Eighth Avenue between Fortieth and Forty-second Street had mobs of people feeding back into Times Square and beyond. The scene was the same at Penn Station six blocks south, and Grand Central Station in Midtown, at Forty-second and Park, over time these masses merged becoming one huge horde of people. Were it not for the massive mobilization of the NYPD and the National Guard, surely the cases of isolated violence would have turned into full-scale riots.

Tonya Johnson, a single mother with her six-year-old son, Kobe, was among the throng of people at Penn Station, and she was one of the few who was exactly where she was supposed to be. Not typically one to make her voice heard, she was fighting for her son. Never underestimate the power of a mother protecting her child.

She had her pass for transport from Penn Station. Such a document was issued to most New Yorkers who were "in the system"—that is, registered with the city's evacuation authority as directed. Sadly, that was true for only 30 percent of the city's residents.

When a man tried to steal her pass, Tonya beat him down with the umbrella she'd brought solely for that purpose, creating a commotion that drew the attention of a nearby armed Guardsman, a thick man of Irish ancestry known by his compatriots affectionately as "Bull." He grabbed the umbrella on the upswing and took one look at the terrified Tonya and realized she was the victim.

"Miss, you can't go around beating the living tar out of folks. So what's going on here?"

The man who'd tried to steal the pass started screaming she'd gone nuts and was attacking him trying to get ahead in line. Bull, seeing the pass in the man's hand, asked to see it. When the man resisted, Bull sternly said, "Hand it over or I'm going to do a lot more than beat you with an umbrella."

Reading it quickly, he handed it back to Tonya and asked if that was her son standing next to her, which she confirmed. Addressing the man, Bull said, "Drop to your knees, put your hands on your head." He approached the man from behind and used one knee to push him forward while he holstered his pistol, and took one of the hundred or so nylon zip ties from his pocket to bind the man's wrists. Then he picked him up, literally throwing him to his feet.

Bull then told Tonya, "Pick up your son and grab my belt with your free hand and don't let go, miss!" He pushed the man in front, literally using him as a shield while yelling, "Make a hole! Make way! Prisoner coming through!" The whole point was not only to subdue the one man but make him an example to those thinking they could take advantage of the chaos.

He reached the entrance to Penn Station on Seventh Avenue, a long flight of stairs leading down into a labyrinth that is a combined shopping mall and train station. Bull pushed ahead and handed Tonya's pass to the first guard controlling access to the stairs. "Miss, you can go ahead," said Bull, as he pushed the man off to the side. There another set of guards were taking prisoners in a deliberate show of force designed to provide deterrence. The goal was to have everyone out of the city in twenty-four hours. It was possible. Well publicized too was that those arrested would be last to leave.

If it came down to the last train, ferry, or bus out of town and there was no more room, those prisoners would be left to whatever fate befell them.

It was a scene repeated dozens of times, but surprisingly not anywhere near as much as the authorities had first feared.

While this small drama was unfolding in NYC, by some miracle, the NSA satellite caught the car on I-95 in Newark—trying to go against the reverse traffic flow—on its way into the Lincoln Tunnel from New Jersey. This was one of the cars purchased by a sleeper agent, who had a hard time getting the dealership to finally release the car (he couldn't provide proof of insurance). The agent was desperately trying to get the car to its intended location near Time Square in the midst of an evacuation. It was clear the thirty-year-old sleeper agent from Syria would never succeed in his mission—to get the car into the heart of the city when every bit of traffic was flowing *out*—yet he was hell-bent on trying. A strategy doomed to failure, which revealed the illogical desperation of a zealot.

From the satellite image, the law enforcement vehicles looked like a pack of wolves descending upon the Spark as it attempted its move into NYC. Air support, of course, arrived first, followed by land vehicles. Eventually, police, military, and FBI vehicles and choppers surrounded the bomb-containing car. There was simply no exit and no surrender. The fear, of course, was the driver could activate the bomb—even though authorities had been assured by the CIA this wasn't possible; but no one liked to trust that kind of intelligence with their lives.

The circle of law enforcement closed rapidly. The driver had been fighting his way against traffic when he heard the helicopters overhead. He knew he'd been caught for sure when the traffic suddenly cleared, leaving him an empty highway. He knew the road was blocked ahead. He mashed the gas pedal to the floor and the car reached its top speed of 112 miles per hour. While capable of such a speed on a road with no incline, the Spark's suspension, tires and steering capabilities were being pushed beyond their limits, and the car was most certainly not under control.

Any slight jerk of the wheel or decent-sized pothole and this chase would end badly. The driver had already made up his mind that he was not going to be caught. Capture, prosecution and punishment at the hands of the infidels was not an option.

Looking ahead, he noticed the roadblock beyond a bridge where the road he was on passed over another highway. He thought, *Why the hell do the Americans always put a roadblock on the opposite side of a bridge? Do they truly think that's going to stop someone?* It does, of course, because most people want to live. In this case, though he'd not been known as a suicide bomber, no one could see the slight widening of his eyes: the expression of one who has come to a realization. This is the look of someone who believes he or she has just gotten a message from God—the fanatical zeal of faith reaffirmed. There was no question he would take this to the end.

The distance to the bridge was closing fast at this speed. The choppers could see he wasn't slowing down. One of them lowered in front of the car, enough to be visible and provide a warning, but the driver did not ease off the accelerator. The chopper dipped lower, coming within a few feet of the car's windshield. The driver's eyes were fixed on the road, and he showed no response whatsoever to the helicopter.

The pilot was able to see the man's face and knew he'd never surrender. He radioed command, requesting orders. The order was clear. If you have a shot, take it. He communicated the orders to the shooter hanging out the open door of the chopper, an expert aerial marksman. The marksman aimed, steadied and, as he slowly exhaled his breath, squeezed the trigger of the M39 EMR.

The driver's head jerked back, hitting the headrest now covered with blood spattered from the exit wound, then slumped to the left, coming to rest on the driver's side window. His eyes were still fixed and staring ahead. Death was instantaneous. As his foot slipped off the accelerator, the car quickly slowed but was still going in excess of seventy miles per hour. It began to swerve left, and the sudden deceleration forced the pursuing officers to take evasive action. One of them passed on the right and positioned his car in front of the Spark. He slowed to allow contact to be made, then gently braked his car.

Despite the fact the police car's driver was an expert at gentle braking, the Spark's steering obviously could not be controlled, and the inevitable rotation could not be avoided. It turned sideways in a perfect ninety-degree hard left and began a new course headed across the median.

The collision into the side of an all-black government-issue Chevrolet Tahoe was a near perfect hit on that vehicle's rear axle, crushing the Spark's front end like an accordion all the way back to the bottom of the windshield. Minor injuries were suffered by the agents.

What looked to be a hundred vehicles from every conceivable law enforcement agency arrived before the dust could settle. Everyone was very glad that road had been closed off, and people needing to use it to evacuate now could be told to go home.

Within minutes, four helicopters landed near the crashed vehicles. One of them, a medevac, evacuated the survivors and the dead sleeper agent. Another chopper contained the bomb squad. Immediately inspecting the car, then taking into consideration the number of people in the area, they determined it would be safer to transport the crashed vehicle than attempt to disarm it here.

Marines used Geiger counters to check for any radiation leakage and found all readings to be minimal. The tiny car was dragged onto an army tilt bed tank transporter—complete overkill for the size of the Spark—that was nearby after dropping off a tank to encourage orderly evacuation. The car was covered and sent on its way to Earle Naval Weapons Station in Monmouth County, New Jersey, where the weapon would be defused and dismantled.

With all the chaos of the past few days, the highway chase wouldn't warrant a report even on the evening news; and while plenty of those witnessing the commotion would have a story to tell, it would remain just that, a story.

Craig's phone beeped and vibrated, signaling a new text message: NEWARK TARGET NEUTRALIZED. NO CAPTIVE. NO INTEL. WEAPON RECOVERED AND SECURED. EVACUATION ENDED.

While it would have been nice to question the target, Craig doubted they would have gotten much new information. He let out a long, cleansing sigh of relief, pleased that one more of the weapons was now accounted for and secured. That it was one of those intended to cause the most human carnage was an additional relief.

JULY 2, 17:15 MDT

Colorado Springs

The car destined for Colorado Springs had gone missing on GM's distribution computers. Rezeya assured them it was most likely a scanning error, that the car would be at the dealership. When the sales manager was paged at Daniels Chevyland in Colorado Springs, like most managers, he didn't take it as urgent.

The flustered receptionist-cashier paged the sales manager a second time, but this time over the speakers came, "God damn it, Harry, get your ass to the parts counter!" Harry heard the stress in her voice, prompting him to quickly take his feet off his desk, return his chair to its upright position and set his coffee cup on a stack of papers where it sloshed out of the cup and all over the paperwork. He was still cursing as he hurried out to the parts counter.

"Where the hell's the fire?" Harry demanded. The frightened receptionist directed her eyes to the two men in black suits. Harry stood before them in the summer uniform of a sales manager for a small new car dealership: short-sleeve ill-fitting polo shirt and light-brown khakis, comfortable loafers and a pair of cellphones clipped to a belt constraining a plentiful gut.

One of them asked, "Are you in charge of this dealership at the moment, or is there an owner here today?"

Harry would have been only too happy to steer these guys to someone else, but regrettably he was the highest-level manager on duty today. "Yeah, the general manager and owner are both off today."

"I'm Special Agent Cross and this is Special Agent Roosevelt, FBI Denver Office," said Cross as both flashed their IDs and badges in a way that offered a glimpse of their guns.

No average citizen is comfortable with FBI agents, and that was no different for Harry. He was racking his brains to figure out what he had done.

"What can I do for you?" was about all he could manage.

"You said the general manager is off today?"

"Yes, sir, he takes Tuesdays off to go golfing with the owner. It's usually a slower day."

"What's your title, then?" asked Agent Cross.

Harry noticed only Agent Cross spoke. Agent Roosevelt was taking notes.

"I'm the sales manager, and I report to the general manager and have authority when he's not here."

"Your name?" asked Agent Cross.

"Harry Weston, sir—er, Harold, but everyone calls me Harry." Automatically he stuck out his hand. Agent Cross looked at it, then back into Harry's face. *All righty then*, thought Harry.

"We are here about a car in your inventory," said Cross.

"You want to buy a car?" asked Harry. It was second nature.

"No, but we need to locate this car immediately. I have a VIN number," said agent Cross.

"OK, let's go to my office. I'll check it out."

The agents followed Harry into his cluttered office, noting the sales board and wondering what the 1s and 1/2s meant. Harry took his seat behind the desk while Roosevelt closed the door behind him.

Harry heard the click of the latch and became agitated, feeling his control was being usurped. He didn't bother offering them seats.

The agents remained standing. To Harry, they were hovering.

"OK, what's the VIN number?" he asked.

"It's K L one C D six six A six K C one zero seven four four nine."

Harry tapped on the keyboard, and the screen popped up with the information: a 2019 Chevrolet Spark, red LT sedan, followed by TRADED 7/01/19.

"Oh, yeah," Harry said, "I remember this car. We traded it while it was en route to us. It was never delivered to the store."

Cross was confused and wondered if this was why the GM location system had lost track of the car; but for now he asked, "What do you mean *traded?*"

"A nearby dealer had a buyer for that car and offered to trade us with a car in his inventory so he could make the sale. We do it all the time, though not so much while the car is *en route*. We usually get a more desirable vehicle for our inventory."

"I see," said Cross, still not clear about the details. "Where is the car now?"

With a shrug, Harry said, "Unless it's been delivered, it's still at that dealership, but usually with a trade it goes right to the customer."

Not the scenario Cross wished to contemplate. Impounding a car from a dealership is one thing; seizing a brand-new car from a citizen would be damn complicated.

Remembering that most of these cars were ordered by customers, Cross asked, "Wasn't this an ordered car? Don't you also have a sale for it?"

"Yeah, but I called the customer myself. When we knew the car was on its way and got the call for the trade, the number had been disconnected. No longer in service. Can't understand why the guy would disappear. He had a one-thousand-dollar deposit and everything. But since we couldn't contact him, I approved the trade."

"I need you to call that dealership. Find out if the car is still there, and then put the guy on hold so I can give you further instructions."

Harry picked up the phone and called the manager at Burt Chevrolet in Parker, Colorado, a suburb of Denver some sixty miles away.

"Yeah, hey Pete, it's Harry at Daniels. You know that Spark we did the trade on? Do you still have it around?"

Harry was nodding and saying *uh huh* and *yeah*, then asked Pete if he could put him on hold.

"OK, he still has the car," Harry explained to the agents. "Says something about it being scratched in transit, so it's still on the lot waiting for the body shop to fix it."

Cross breathed a huge sigh of relief, motioned for the receiver. Without salutation Cross said, "Listen carefully. This is Special Agent Cross with the FBI. I want you to lock that car up, out of sight, in your service bay. Don't do anything with it. Close the dealership, send everyone home. And I mean *everyone*, except for you."

Harry looked at Cross as though he'd lost his mind. There was no way Pete would do any such thing. Managers are constantly playing jokes on one another, partly to build comradery and partly through sheer boredom.

Pete just laughed into the receiver. "Good one. Tell Harry he's really gone off the deep end."

"Pete, is it?" asked Cross.

"Yes, who *is* this?" Pete asked with a more than impatient tone.

"I've given you my name, Pete, you've seen the president's address to the nation, you know what's going on, right?" asked Cross.

A much more contrite Pete responded, "Yeah. But he never mentioned Colorado at all."

"No, that's right, he didn't, he had been assured we would have this threat neutralized and didn't see the need to alarm people here. Now do as I've instructed, we'll be there in less than an hour."

"Yeah, yeah, I've got it, but don't you want to speak with the owner, Mr. Ramsey?"

Cross cursed himself for not asking in the first place. "If he's there, absolutely, I want to speak with him."

The phone began to play music. Pete never said anything like *sure, hold on please,* he just pressed Hold.

Cross became extremely agitated.

Minutes passed. No doubt there'd be confused and curious discussion between Pete and the owner; three minutes turned to four. Cross had mere seconds to decide his next move when the phone clicked and Mr. Ramsey picked up on the other end.

Neil Ramsey—he still considered "Mr." his dad—at thirty-six was the third-generation owner of Burt Chevrolet. He was capable, not entitled, with a natural humility.

"Hello, this is Neil Ramsey, and I have to tell you right up front I was skeptical of even taking this call."

"I can appreciate that, though you're a smart man, as I am sure you pondered the potential consequences of *not* taking the call?" Cross countered.

"Yes, sir, indeed, especially with the news today. Now about the car?" asked Neil.

"Mr. Ramsey"—Neil interrupted and asked to be called Neil—"OK, Neil. If you don't do precisely as I say, you will be surrounded by more police, FBI, and military in twenty minutes than you ever dreamed possible, and they will carry out the instructions I already gave Pete. Do we understand each other?"

"I would never be uncooperative, I don't think there's even a choi—"

"Yes or no!"

"What do I do?"

"Close your store. Send everyone home but you stay. Tell them a bomb threat has been called in. That will explain our presence there in the next few minutes. Get them out!"

"OK, that's easy, what else?"

"The car I discussed with your manager: I only told him part of the truth. There's no time to fill you in. That car is dangerous and we need to recover it now. Your financial loss will be handled, how exactly, I don't know," Cross explained.

"Can you hold the line for a minute please?" The line clicked and the canned music came back on. Cross held the receiver in front of his face and stared at it in disbelief.

Neil was back in less than a minute. "Everyone is going home. They are already leaving. The car will be in the service shop. Have your people come directly to the service bay door number four. I will be the only person here and will let them in. You guys take what you need. Just leave me a number of someone to contact. Not to be selfish, but I do have a business—"

"I understand."

Neil heard a click and the line went dead.

JULY 3, 10:00 EDT

Washington, D.C.

After the car in New York had been located and neutralized, residents there were directed to return home as quickly as possible. It was utter chaos, since the National Guard troops and basically all but the NYPD had been pulled out and moved south to help execute the final evacuation of Washington, D.C.

With just fourteen hours left until the anticipated detonation, the acting director of Homeland Security reallocated all resources from Boston south to Richmond, Virginia, to descend upon D.C. to begin evacuation.

To be in the metro Washington, D.C., region, no matter what the media—TV, radio, podcast or web video, the same message from President Barton was played on a loop, and even text messages were sent to every reachable mobile phone. It was a communications blackout and total success thanks to lessons learned after 9/11.

"This is President Barton. The region of Washington, D.C., including its suburbs, is hereby ordered to evacuate. This is not a drill. This is not voluntary. This is a mandatory evacuation. If you are hearing this message, you should be leaving the region. Your goal is to move at least one hundred miles either west, north or south. Let me repeat: all movement needs to be west, north, or south only. Anyone going east will be arrested. Those who are on the Delmarva Peninsula are requested to go north. Do not stop until you reach at least Philadelphia. If you are located west of the Chesapeake Bay, all roads leading out of the area will be using both sides of the road. Follow the instructions of the authorities. I have declared the United States to be under martial law. You can and will be arrested without any due process."

Door-to-door, local police and National Guard personnel were using military-spec infrared and ultrasonic sound detection. If any door went unopened and there was indication of life inside, the door was busted down.

There are two reasons someone would be holed up and not evacuating as ordered. The first is innocuous: he or she incapacitated and can't get to the door, or is suspicious of authority, not sure those in charge can be trusted; and the person's beliefs, depending, can range from mild mistrust to schizophrenic paranoia. The second class largely consists of criminals holed up to guard their inventory, ranging from stolen electronics to valuable property to illegal arms and drugs.

Orders were orders: no one was to remain in the city. The options were leave on your own, leave with assistance if you couldn't leave on your own, or—lastly, leave in custody.

No one knew the true reason why people were being evacuated, but rumors were rampant and they weren't often wrong. Still, there's an element of hope in the thought that knowledge is uncertain.

Dark conjecture, through word of mouth, often leads to panic. An emergency can bring out the best and the worst in us. When life is in the balance, people are capable of just about anything. Panic may be helpful too in lighting a fire under people's asses. Making a ghost town out of an area thirty miles in every direction from the Washington Monument in a period of twenty-four hours wouldn't have been possible without a hefty dose of it.

JULY 3, 11:30 PDT

Las Vegas

When President Barton called the governor of Nevada a little before midnight on July 2 to explain the situation, he ordered the complete and total evacuation of southern Nevada, and he thought the order would be carried out. The governor declined federal assistance, in no small part because he carelessly didn't agree with the threat assessment. He was a member of both classes of resisters: he didn't trust the administration, and he had every intention of protecting the interests of a group of casino operators whose stated desire was to "let things be."

As such, thanks to the governor's lack of action and failure to engage the Emergency Broadcast System, the citizens of Las Vegas were not issued warnings.

Las Vegas has a population of roughly one million, but that number can swell to more than three million when the city's hotels are near to capacity. This happens every Fourth of July, when despite the oppressive heat, there is rarely an empty room to be found.

People in their homes who were watching the news did begin an exodus. Geographically, Las Vegas is a horrible city to evacuate. Interstate 15 is the main artery out of southern Nevada. While Highway 95 can handle some traffic over the Hoover Dam and into Arizona, that route had been closed for fear the dam was a target. Going south, I-15 narrows from three lanes to two, creating a bottleneck famous for causing traffic jams 100 miles long. Going north is the same: beyond the city boundary the road is two lanes in each direction. Even using reverse flow, evacuating people in time would be an almost insurmountable difficulty.

Worst of all was the challenge of getting two million visitors to safety who had arrived on flights and used taxis.

Lack of routes is hardly the problem when people don't know they are supposed to be leaving. By 5:30 P.M., far too many tourists hadn't heard the news; the casinos notoriously block cell phones on the casino floor. The only way the message to evacuate was getting around was by word of mouth, and that only served to create a panic. When people started to notice casino employees leaving, it all became real and panic spread. The situation was fast becoming dangerous.

At 6 P.M., the president asked the governor about the progress of the evacuation. He told the governor he was very disappointed to learn that many of the available aircraft had left with less than two-thirds their capacity. Further, he was amazed to learn that the casinos had not stopped operations and evacuated their guests.

At 6:15 P.M., President Barton informed the governor of Nevada that Colonel Jack Robbins, commander of Nellis Air Force Base would be taking over. At that moment, twelve armed soldiers entered the governor's office and President Barton explained to him over the phone, "These men are here to arrest you. You are being charged with treason." And with that he hung up.

Once troops were in place and could direct both pedestrian and vehicular traffic, the commander ordered all power cut to the Las Vegas strip and to any casino located off the strip. As elevators no longer worked, people were to use the stairs. It went much faster.

No car was allowed to enter a lane to the Interstate not at full capacity. Anyone dumb enough to refuse someone transport would be put in restraints and a stranger ordered to drive. Once a safe distance was reached, the ex-driver would be taken into custody.

People in the United States had never been under martial law. They had no clue that in that moment, civil rights do not exist. It was akin to being a prisoner of war, a concept most could barely comprehend.

At last, the cars were on the road. The monster hotels, some with more than five thousand rooms, were emptying out and I-15 came to a standstill.

Traffic stopped. Police and media helicopters confirmed that traffic was almost entirely choked from as far away as San Bernardino, California. It was a parking lot. Off-road trucks and SUVs were trying their luck on the shoulder and in the medians, only to find themselves inevitably at an impasse, some obstacle that prevented them from going any further.

It was at this point the military personnel were called in from Fort Irwin just outside of Barstow, California. Their mission: to create the world's largest parking lot in the desert around Baker, California.

JULY 3, 23:20 EDT

Washington, D.C.

The car in Washington, D.C., would never be found. The terrorists had planned the location of that car for more than a decade. They had placed a sleeper agent as an employee at the embassy of the Republic of Tunisia. It was someone at a low enough level he or she would never be looked at too closely, but high enough to have parking privileges in the embassy's underground parking area.

While subterranean placement of the bomb wasn't ideal—it would severely lower the blast radius—it was better than to risk it being discovered. An embassy is considered the sovereign territory of the country to which it belongs. Even under martial law, no law enforcement agency of the United States would have the right to enter any foreign embassy.

While all the embassies within the evacuation zone did manage to get their people to safety, what precise vehicles were parked in their secure facilities was unknown. It was a brilliant plan.

The location of the Tunisian embassy was the reason it was selected. Located at 1515 Massachusetts Avenue NW, the embassy was barely more than half a mile from the front door of the White House.

Being the epicenter of the blast that occurred precisely at 12:01 A.M. on July 4, the square-shaped boring white building with pale green exterior louvers covering the windows and a green iron fence wrapped around its lawn—was nothing but a massive hole. In a virtually perfect circular pattern around the site more than a half mile in diameter was debris, ranging from small fragments in the center to large parts of mostly standing buildings at the outer edge.

The embassies of Australia, El Salvador, and the Philippines were destroyed, as was the landmark Metropolitan AME Church and National City Christian Church.

Numerous hotels, apartments, institutes, and museums were laid to ruin, in the quarter mile diameter of the epicenter.

Hundreds of other structures at the outer part of the half-mile diameter suffered severe damage, including the White House. While it was still very much recognizable, it was devastated, mostly by being rained on by massive chunks of debris. Even farther outside the destruction zone there was serious damage. The Washington Monument, even with the reinforcements it had recently undergone, was no match for the shock wave and falling debris, which caused it to blow apart.

The majority of Washington's other monuments and the Capitol Building suffered significant damage, most of which could not be repaired without major reconstruction; it would take years and billions of dollars before Washington, D.C., would be the place people once knew. That was if the radiation didn't dictate it could never be inhabited again.

JULY 3, 23:30 PDT

Las Vegas

The FBI was conducting a floor-to-floor search of every parking garage in Las Vegas. The NSA's supercomputer was not finding the Chevy Spark that had been picked up two days earlier by the customer who had ordered it back in April.

Evidently, just as in Washington D.C., the car was not in an open space or in a place where it could be seen from the sky. A severe limitation of the NSA's program, "Eyes in the Sky" can't see into garages, houses or buildings unless it knows what specific house or building to "look" into.

Even then, if the resources are directed to a particular building or house, they are directed to listen and search for heat wave patterns that are signatures of human beings, not cold cars sitting parked.

As midnight approached, it was becoming more and more clear that this car would not be found. There was nothing anyone could do; the manpower was not available to search room to room to ensure the evacuation of the city. It was estimated that the evacuation of Las Vegas had been less than 90 percent complete.

If the intelligence was correct—and based on the explosion in Washington, D.C., there was no reason to believe it was not—a nuclear blast would occur somewhere in Las Vegas in approximately thirty minutes.

Craig Stout was on the SAT link with Colonel Jack Robbins. Since Robbins had been volunteered by President Barton to take charge of the Las Vegas evacuation, it had been clear the incompetence of the governor ultimately would cost thousands of people their lives.

"Jack, what the fuck is happening? Our satellite recon indicates heat sources that are consistent with human forms in the city *in the thousands.* Is this shit right?"

"Your eyes don't deceive you. I am afraid the delay these numbnuts caused is not something we are going to be able to entirely recover from," said the colonel. "Furthermore, as you know, our staffing at Nellis isn't huge, and most of them are trained to fly, not handle ground operations of this sort. The men from Irwin have been leading, directing my men with what to do, and there were some turf wars until I cracked a few heads."

"But ... where are we? How many are still in harm's way?"

"My estimate is three hundred thousand," the colonel answered. "In a little fewer than five hours we've managed to get two and a half million people to what is considered a safe area. And, sir, I sure as hell hope it is a safe area, given that many of them are baking in the California desert at the moment!"

Craig grumbled, exhausted and defeated. "We can only do our best. At some point our human limitations are met, and then all we can do is hope. I am not a spiritual man as you may or may not know ... but at this point even I have to say ... it's in God's hands."

"Not spiritual, hell, you're a goddamn heathen! But sir, there is no one I'd rather be taking orders from on this one." The colonel's words rang in Craig's ears as a source of pride; he still had dreams of hearing such praise from his father.

"Thank you, Robbins. Now I need to know when you guys have to ditch."

"Sir, it's your call. I don't go until the job is done. I'm not going till you give the order."

"Yeah, I was afraid of that," said Craig. He had to weigh 300,000 lives against the odds of getting the heroes who were trying to save them out in time. No matter what he chose, untold thousands were going to die, and there was no point in further loss of life by keeping the evacuation teams on any longer.

Craig's voice was raspy. His head hung low as he asked, "What's the plan for your men?"

"Fort Irwin's men need ten minutes to get to safety. They'll blast across the desert in Humvees. My men have choppers and we have room for the FBI guys, and they all need five minutes to reach the choppers, two minutes to take off, and five minutes to reach safety. They all have a go command on my word."

Craig looked at the clock: T-minus twenty-four minutes. He gave the order. "Get all evacuation teams out now. And Colonel, when I say now, I mean it. No fucking heroics, are we clear?"

Craig couldn't see it but the colonel saluted. "Crystal clear, sir!"

Robbins was familiar with death. He was trained to accept loss of life as part of combat, but not civilian life. That was never acceptable. "And the rest of the people?" he whispered.

"We've done all we can do. That will have to rest on the shoulders of those who caused the delay."

"Yes, sir. God help them," said Robbins, noting his use of *them* was not at all clear.

JULY 4, 12:01 A.M.

Las Vegas, Nevada

For the past three hours, from living rooms and coffee shops to bars and sidewalks where one can see a television, people were transfixed and frozen, staring at screens, staring at their phones that were flooded with images of similar scenes, beginning with what occurred at one-minute past midnight Eastern Daylight Time, 2,426 miles away.

Nearly everyone across the globe was equally transfixed, silently waiting and wondering if it would really happen to Las Vegas, too. Suddenly, the flash of light temporarily blinded the cameras and the satellite transmission went to snow. Slowly, the picture returned with the telltale mushroom cloud in the sky and the world stood still.

A blinding flash followed by a vacuum in space that seemed to stop time, silence, then an expansion of air, with a percussive force so massive it signaled the end of everything. For the people in this moment in this place in the universe, it *was* the end of everything. A force so strong and powerful, it seemed it could only have come from God Himself.

This is what thousands of people saw and felt at 12:01 A.M., July 4. They were the lucky ones, as that is all they saw and felt. A glimpse of white light, accompanied by a brief sensation of a rush of hot wind: a force that instantly overcame them with an expanding energy that consumed their being.

The bronze glass of the sail-shaped structure of the Wynn Casino was first shattered on the west side as the force of the blast blew out walls, furniture, televisions, and beds—some complete with their sleeping occupants—through the glass on the east side of the building. For moments, a twisted iron and concrete skeleton of the building stood virtually empty before it too finally groaned and screeched as it crashed to the ground under its own weight.

The massive Venetian and Palazzo hotels were two of the terrorists' primary targets: the only casinos on the Las Vegas strip owned by a Jew and therefore the most meaningful to destroy. The Venetian's thirty-five stories of concrete, iron, glass and marble crumbled under the shock wave of the blast. The Palazzo, being newer, fared only slightly better.

Moments before, just down the strip, an innocent-looking Chevrolet Spark was parked on the fourth level of the self-parking structure of the Harrah's Hotel and Casino. Since September 11, security had been tight at the Venetian and Palazzo casinos and all entering vehicles were subject to inspection, much to the annoyance of taxi and limo drivers, who have to go through the process even for drop-offs. This meant that the Spark had to be parked at the nearby Harrah's even though it was not the intended location. It was close enough, though, to do the damage desired.

At the epicenter of the blast was Harrah's and its neighbor, the LINQ Hotel, better known by its former name, the Imperial Palace, now a pile of dust and rubble. All that remained of the tacky and dated Mardi Gras were small parts of its iconic clowns.

Famous for its fountains that performed in synch to songs such as "Luck Be a Lady," the water of the lake in front of the Bellagio Hotel was blown out and vaporized. The empty cement crater was later filled with debris from the atomized buildings.

Across the boulevard at the Paris Hotel, small parts of the legs of its kitschy Eiffel Tower were the only identifiable remnants of the painstakingly accurate one-half scale replica of the original in Paris.

The devastation continued for nearly a mile in every direction, beyond which there were lessening degrees of damage fanning out at least two miles: Bally's, Barbary Coast, Caesar's, Planet Hollywood, The Mirage, Treasure Island, and the recently opened multibillion-dollar Crystal City hotel-residential-commercial towers all were total losses.

The MGM and Mandalay Bay on the south side of the strip were ruins, and on the north side, the vulnerable Stratosphere's supporting tripod crumbled to dust, plummeting the huge sphere to earth.

The failure to fully evacuate the strip in time was evidenced by the sickening sight of human bodies and, more horrifically, body parts spread far and wide like grotesque litter.

They will soon ... her words floated back to Craig, who woke from a trance into a nightmare. *They just choose never to acknowledge.*

EPILOGUE

While the terror of *what if* resides in all of us, I remain compelled to remember this guidance from one of the men in history I most respect, Benjamin Franklin, who wrote, as early as 1755, "Those who would give up essential Liberty, to purchase a little temporary Safety, deserve neither Liberty nor Safety."

ACKNOWLEDGMENTS

Barbara Tipton, mother of my best friend, Jim, who bravely took on reading this book in its early stages to provide advice on grammar and structure. Her support and encouragement greatly helped.

Donald Lucas, my ex-husband, who tolerated all the hours with my nose in my laptop while we were supposed to be enjoying a show together. Sadly, it was a meager example of how I should have been more attentive.

Marjorie Lucas (Mom), Don's mother, who genuinely believes I can do anything, even though it's not true. (Isn't that the definition of motherly?)

Michael Wilde and *Kelly Tomkies*, my editors, each of whom provided wise guidance and many, many corrections!

Michael Dobrin, a fellow writer, who encouraged and helped me gain access to the Benicia, CA, port and vehicle processing facility.

Larry Brown, who helped me visit the Long Beach, CA, port and vehicle processing facility.

Hyundai Motor, for graciously being my host on my several trips to Korea as an automotive journalist over the past twenty-five years.

"David M", for taking me to the gym at Pope Air Force Base, where I saw the lay of the land and made up the rest.

Tonya Munden, *Troy Turner*, *Tiffiny* Dunn, my siblings. No matter what, they always have my back, even when it's not at all comfortable for them.

Susan Turner, my supportive and kind stepmom, and Richard Price, her husband and a voracious reader who I hope enjoys this book.

Kristy Roberts, a dear friend, who early on proofread pages, shielding me from numerous embarrassments.

AUTHOR'S NOTE

Ten years prior to the tragic events of 9/11 I was on a flight taking off from John F. Kennedy International Airport. It was on Good Friday, one of those wonderful, bright, clear, sunny spring days when New Yorkers rejoice that winter is over. As we climbed, we had a brilliant view of the New York City skyline and I had a thought: What if a plane flew into those towers?

When it happened, it occurred to me afterward, *What if I had written that?* I couldn't help but wonder if such a fiction might have served as a warning.

I've spent most of my adult life working in the automotive industry; I've toured car factories from Alabama to Korea, and something has always bothered me about how cars are imported all over the world.

Prior to 9/11, cargo freight came into this country without much scrutiny. In the years since, there are tighter controls on freight that is shipped in containers, including random scans for radioactive isotopes common with what might be found in a nuclear bomb or a dirty bomb. Yet, the thousands of imported cars are driven off ships and parked at port processing facilities for distribution inland with very little inspection. This book pursues a what-if scenario: What's the worst that could happen?

.

www.ingramcontent.com/pod-product-compliance
Lightning Source LLC
Chambersburg PA
CBHW051518170626
46811CB00002B/880